Daybreak

Nightfall

Book One

Jeffery Martin Botzenhart

Solstice Publishing - www.solsticepublishing.com

Copyright 2017 – Jeffery Martin Botzenhart

Daybreak

Nightfall – Book One

By

Jeffery Martin Botzenhart

Dedication

For my brother Jim.

When we were kids, he was the pilot of our red Radio Flyer
wagon speeding down our Grandma's hill. Though gone
for many years now, he's still our pilot, guiding us on
through our beloved memories of him.

Part One
Dawn

Chapter One

"Five—four—three—two—one." With the overhead thunderous roar of the city tram deafening him, he shielded his eyes from the blinding flicker of the lights and a cloud of stirred up dust. Tossing his backpack up over the metal fence, Sebastian winced as he felt a slight pain from the disrupted electrical charge surging through the chain links. Climbing as quickly as he could, he silently counted off the seconds to the top, jumping off a split-second before the full charge returned.

Landing awkwardly on his feet, he fell to the ground, grasping his ankle. The throbbing radiated through his whole foot but he didn't think he had broken it. *"Rats,"* he growled in pain, catching his breath. Pulling down the hood of his jacket, he cautiously glanced around, hoping no one had seen him climb the fence. Close to midnight, he wasn't really worried about it, as most of the people living in this part of the city were sound asleep by ten or eleven. As for the city surveillance cameras, that was another story. They were everywhere even in places you would least expect them to be. The authorities claimed their need to protect the cities warranted such extensive security, but Sebastian thought different. To him, the cameras were a means of control far beyond what should have been acceptable. But terrorism, cyberattacks, and hate have a way of warping minds into submission with unrealistic promises of safety.

Slowly standing up, Sebastian put weight on his ankle. It still hurt but he knew he would deal with it. After pulling out a small flashlight from his backpack, a sly smile crept over his face while standing there surrounded by heaping piles of junk. Everything imaginable, from old tires and refrigerators to worn clothes and broken televisions, were neatly strewn about in piles. The rubber smell was overpowering, but Sebastian breathed in the air corrupted with other scents, not pungent like garbage, but more industrial. Wandering over to the nearest pile, he picked up an old machine he remembered seeing in a picture, something called a typewriter. A few of the letters stuck and the ribbon was missing, yet it seemed to be in decent shape and possibly might still work. Finding a replacement ribbon would be a problem. He didn't know where to even begin looking for something like that.

Returning the typewriter to the pile, Sebastian continued on to a stack he recognized. From his pocket, he removed his reading glasses, putting them on as he approached. He reached out grabbing hold of a book. Roughly, ten years ago the printing of books had been outlawed for so-called environmental reasons regarding the preservation of trees. From that moment on, all publications were done so electronically. Being that the majority of the public had been reading books and newspapers with mobile devices for years, few challenged this change. Only libraries and bookstores suffered as new printed books were no longer made available. With their funding and profits cut due to readers abandoning their once popular locations, many closed. Over time, even collectors shied away from purchasing books as their value declined. Sebastian, however, picked up one after another, awed as if discovering a lost treasure.

Sitting down on what once was a comfortable recliner, he read title after title, recognizing some and wondering over others he'd never heard the names of. Realizing he could only take a few with him, Sebastian selected three stories of authors he hadn't read, stuffing these books into his backpack before getting up.

Dump sites around San Francisco's perimeter were highly regarded as blight to city officials, yet they were necessary for the disposal of things deemed trash. Sebastian viewed places such as this as cultural museums holding long forgotten pieces of the past. As he continued wandering here and there, he noticed many objects that had been coveted and desired by older generations. Boom boxes sat next to the record players they replaced, with cassettes, vinyl records, and CD's littering the ground. Cellular phones, some models appearing ancient, were heaped upon old dial telephones. Appliances, clothing, furniture, all from one era to the next, were similarly displayed. What stuck Sebastian most was that pretty much everything in sight might still be of use but was discarded simply because it wasn't new and improved.

Sebastian approached the area he was most interested in visiting. Lining both sides of an alley, a dozen or so arcade games, ranging from pinball machines to alien-destroying video game favorites stood like sentinels waiting to be brought to life. All, except one. Placed at the very end, this glass chamber appeared similar to a wind tunnel machine, briefly popular in shopping malls decades ago. But there was something unique in its construction, leading Sebastian to believe it held a different purpose. With a card swipe, a number pad, and two pairs of headphones, more than anything else it resembled either an old telephone booth or a confined space, big enough for two, possibly for the purpose of listening to music. Since first seeing it a week ago, Sebastian wanted nothing more than to open the glass door and climb in. Yet not understanding what it could do kept him from further exploring it.

As he reached the center of the alley, a glaring floodlight turned on. Scurrying under one of the larger pinball machines, he held his breath, waiting for someone to step out of the adjacent brick building. The loud banging of a door followed the metallic whining of hinges with a deep male voice calling out, "Is anyone there?" Black-skinned bare feet stepped into view just down from Sebastian's hiding place. Swallowing hard, the back of his neck prickling, he waited in tense agony, expecting to be caught. A moment later, the feet turned away with the door soon slamming and the alley returning to darkness.

Exhaling his relief, Sebastian crawled out from his hiding place, dusting off cobwebs clinging to his jacket. With one more cautious glance around, once satisfied he was alone, he stalked off back toward the fence. Checking the time on his watch, he intended to be ready to climb the fence once the next tram crossed the overhead tracks. However, he noticed something to his right, altering his escape plan. A strong breeze slightly moved an unlocked gate just down from where he stood. Anxious not to be seen, he spied around and then bolted toward it.

Once standing outside, Sebastian covered his ears, muffling the sound of the tram. It sped by, leaving a thick cloud of dust and dirt in its wake. Coughing out for fresh air, he then adjusted his backpack on his shoulders. Partly glancing back at the fence, his body quaked in fear, his stomach growing nauseous in noticing the gate now secured and locked and a barefoot, black male teen walking away toward the building.

***

Climbing up a fire escape an hour later, Sebastian unsteadily leaned against a wall once he reached the roof. In perfect view before him, his eye looked out at the impressive skyscrapers of downtown San Francisco, the realm of the city elite displaying glass towers glistening with the moon's reflection and shimmering with lights from within. Trams sped along carrying privileged passengers to luxurious destinations and events. He seldom wondered what it would be like to venture there and witness a world shielded from the lower classes living in the surrounding districts. To him, this modern San Francisco seemed as alien as old pictures of the Martian frontier.

Sighing with exhaustion, he walked over to a metal door and opened it. Turning on a dim light he disappeared inside. A month ago he claimed this abandoned utility room as his home after escaping from a boys shelter house two districts away. On shelves where tools and gallons of paint once sat, Sebastian now had an impressive collection of books he had salvaged from trash heaps and dump sites around the city. He'd read every one, the works of Charles Dickens being his favorite. Reaching into his backpack, he withdrew three new books to add to his private library, resolving to begin reading J.D. Salinger's *The Catcher in the Rye* before closing his eyes for the night.

Although the utility room was small, having only enough space for his shelves and a cot he found, it did happen to have one important extra feature, a bathroom with a toilet and sink. Lacking hot running water, it served its purpose, allowing him to be clean and offering drinking water. Shedding his clothes, he stepped into a makeshift shower he built using a hose. Trembling under the frigid water he quickly washed and then dried off.

Looking into a cracked mirror hung above the sink, his sixteen-year-old reflection didn't match how he felt inside as if he'd already lived an entire lifetime. He was tired, having little energy left. And the hollowness in his stomach was not just about missed meals, but maybe about loneliness too. Reaching up, Sebastian ran his fingers through his feathery, short brown hair and looked at the redness near his soft gray eyes. While brushing his teeth, he grinned, remembering something he had overheard someone say. *Smile every day, even if there isn't anything to smile about.*

Dressing in black gym shorts, Sebastian eased down on the cot, propping the pillow up behind him. Resting his back against the wall, he fetched his reading glasses from his backpack and picked up his book. Opening his chosen book to chapter one, he only read a few words before his eyes grew too heavy to stay open. The book slipped from his grasp as he fell asleep.

Chapter Two

Gasping for breath with his face breaching the cold water's surface, Sebastian's ears captured high-pitched screaming next to him. Wet and trembling in fear, he wanted to cry out but was too terrified to make a sound. Catching a glimpse in front of himself, he saw dark water pouring into the car from the shattered windshield. In the front passenger seat, a woman's head lifelessly floated face up in the rising water. "It's all your fault. It's all your fault." He kept hearing from a frightened voice bellowing next to him. The voice then wailed, "*Daddy, Daddy!*"

Another voice, much deeper, groaned out, "*My— son.*" He couldn't see who was talking. There was something plunging into the murky water next to him, his eyes were doused as he felt his body being dragged away from the panicked voices.

Screaming out, Sebastian awakened, sitting up. With his heaving chest throbbing, he fought to catch his breath with his surroundings clearing through his sleep-blurred vision. Taking his glasses off and setting them on the bookshelf, he rubbed his eyes. Breathing in, he thought he could still smell the stench from the water which was impossible here in the utility room. Resting his head on his pillow, he understood it was just a nightmare, one he suffered again and again.

It had been two days since Sebastian last dreamt these terrible images. Yet no matter how hard he tried, he couldn't remember anything more, and each time he was left wondering if it was real. He couldn't ever recall riding in a car. It also seemed to have happened a long time ago when he was much younger. The earliest memories he had were of his time at the shelter, constantly being tormented by the older boys. There were many times they would lock him away in a dark room for hours on end, only occasionally coming back, pounding on the door yelling obscenities and threatening to beat him. The worst thing of all, though, happened after being dragged up to the sadistic administrator's office where he was forced to recite profane scripture, with the slightest lack of conviction a punishable offense.

Bursting in tears, Sebastian clenched his eyelids closed, desperately wanting to clear his mind of the remnants of the dream. Wiping away the tears streaming down his cheeks, he sat up staring straight ahead for a moment before looking left and right. For now, this small metal room with no windows would do for his safe place. It just had to.

Rising from the cot, Sebastian walked into the bathroom to grab a drink from the faucet. With the clear water flowing, he leaned his face down, letting the water run over his lips, tasting its coolness. Before turning off the faucet, he lowered his hands into the basin to wet his palms. Touching his face, the nightmare once more flashed in his mind, sending him staggering back away from the sink. Taking several deep breaths, Sebastian struggled to calm down enough to walk back to the sink. His hand trembled as he reached out to turn off the faucet. He hadn't turned on the light when he stepped into the bathroom, but the light from over his bed offered enough illumination to show his reflection in the mirror as a dark quivering shadow.

Returning to the cot, Sebastian dragged his blanket up to his shoulders. Trying to stop the tremor gripping his hand, he stared up at the ceiling, waiting for it to end. Exhaling away the last of his fear, he forced his mind to think of something else, where his thoughts ended up returning to his visit to the dump site a few hours ago.

Common sense told him not to return after being kind of caught by that boy, roughly his age. But it was one of the few places without security cameras and there was so much left to explore. Thinking of what else he could find there, Sebastian closed his eyes with hopes for a peaceful sleep this time.

***

The new day had been like every other for Sebastian since running away from the San Gabriel Boys Shelter. The morning hours were spent doing odd jobs, earning a few dollars to buy something to eat. Always cautious how much he spent, today he bought a banana, saving the rest of his money to hopefully afford a loaf of bread and peanut butter by the end of the week. By noon, he would be rummaging through dumpsters for metal and glass he could take to recycling centers, again hoping to earn money. With city laws demanding citizens follow recycling programs, he usually found very little, earning practically nothing. The remainder of his day, until just after dark, he spent eluding police. If caught, he would be returned to the shelter house. Given the choice of either the San Gabriel Boys Shelter or death, dying would win out. There was no going back for him.

The afternoon had turned cloudy with steady rain showers and by nine o'clock that night, his jeans and hoodie were soaked. Resisting common sense, Sebastian returned to the dump site he visited the night before. After arriving, he found the gate unlocked and partially open. Ignoring his instinct to leave, he cautiously stepped inside, lured in by the undiscovered treasures waiting for him.

A gust of wind pulled his eyes toward the ground. Dust stirred as he walked. He realized it hadn't rained a drop here at the dump site. The air was hot, not unexpected in July, but warmer than usual. His body ached, the trembling in his hand continuing, consequences of another restless night. Shedding his hoodie, he hoped it and the white T-shirt clinging to his skin would dry soon.

Returning to the stack of books, Sebastian found three more he'd not read, stuffing them into his backpack. One, titled *Interview with a Vampire*, sounded cool. He wandered away, searching through piles of clothing. Sifting through underwear, laughing at some much larger than he'd ever seen, he finally came across shirts and jeans. Finding a few T-shirts his size, he took them with him, packing them with the books.

Wary of approaching the brick building, Sebastian had decided to steer clear of it, but something leaning against the wall caught his attention, forcing him to step forward. Tracing his fingers across the silky smooth surface, he looked with wonder upon a large multicolored kite, the most beautiful thing he'd ever seen. Smiling for a reason he couldn't understand, he just kept staring at it. Taking it with him crossed his mind, but he knew he couldn't, as carrying it across town would draw attention to him.

Stepping back, Sebastian realized where he was. Not intending to go near the alley with the arcade games, the kite had drawn him close. Walking up to the first pinball machine, his fingers traced over the dusty glass, leaving clean marks upon the surface. Wondering what it would be like to play it, his fingers pressed the buttons, even though he knew nothing would happen.

Reeling backward in response to a brilliant flash of lightning and a quaking clap of thunder, Sebastian watched a heavy rainfall at the far end of the dump site, drawing closer to him. Quickly turning, he saw the glass chamber at the end of the alley. Maybe he could get inside it until the rain stopped?

Reaching for the door handle, Sebastian pulled it open as the first raindrops pelted his T-shirt. Once inside, a deluge of rain fell, so heavy he couldn't even see the video games near him. While covering his ears from the intense sounds of the storm, he glanced up, seeing a pair of headphones. Pulling them down, he eased them onto his head, fitting them over his ears, deafening him to the sounds of the thunder.

An explosion of lightning momentarily blinded him, sending an electrical charge surging through the metal frame. Sebastian's eyes grew large as he noticed a red illumination under the keypad and heard a low humming sound through the headphones. An overhead light flickered, followed by a slight jolting pain, like a needle's prick at the back of his head, forcing his eyes closed.

Another flash of lightning had Sebastian opening his eyes. His breath rushed from his lungs with shock when he saw the young black teen standing in the rain just outside the glass case. His dark clothes clearly drenched by the storm, the teen reached over, securing the door of the glass chamber. Suddenly growing drowsy, unable to speak or react in any way, Sebastian's eyelids closed as the sound of a seagull echoed in his ear.

* * *

Hearing a chime from his cell phone, Lee Dryden rolled over in bed miles away at his home in Silicon Valley. Rubbing his eyes, he attempted to focus on the blinking message.

"*Who is it?*" A woman's voice groggily mumbled over his shoulder.

"I don't know," he responded, running his hands over his soft beard, trying to figure out the message. With his eyes more awake, he sat up, his mind jolted by what he read. A message he never imagined seeing again continued flashing on the screen, *Daybreak*.

Bolting out of bed, he rushed out into the hallway, his wife calling after him with words he couldn't comprehend.

Chapter Three

A light spray of water doused Sebastian's face, pulling him from a trance. His eyes grew wide as his jaw dropped, watching turquoise-colored waves crashing in upon the shore, the white foam rolling over the sand, just barely reaching his toes. With continued wonder, he stood up glancing out toward a fog bank, shrouding the unsettled open sea from view. A screech from overhead lured his gaze up at seagulls calling to one another in the gray cloudy sky. And there was another presence, something he clearly remembered. Soaring above, held hostage within the gusting wind, a large multicolored kite shared the sky with the birds. Updrafts forced it higher, then releasing it to spiral down before being recaptured and thrust upward. His eyes followed the string to its source, tethered to a stick buried deep in the shore next to a sandcastle.

Flashing in his mind, the memory of a storm faded, as if it wasn't even real. Deeply breathing in the salty fragrance of the sea, Sebastian stepped forward, watching his feet disappear in the cool seafoam. A pelican then swooped down from the sky, skimming the ocean's surface before diving in capturing a fish for its meal. With a smile bursting across his expression, Sebastian couldn't remember the last time he'd experienced such tranquility in a place.

On a nearby bluff just up the coast, Sebastian spotted the white tower of a lighthouse, the only structure visible from where he stood. Walking in that direction, his eyes watched beach grass blown by the wind and a tattered fence, severely weathered yet holding steadfast amidst the surrounding sand dunes being sculpted by the assaulting gusts.

As he reached the base of the bluff, Sebastian discovered a wooden staircase leading off the beach. Treading barefoot up the steps and a planked walkway, he soon arrived at a white picket fence surrounding an open yard and a small white cottage at the lighthouse's base. Sprigs of wildflowers gently swayed near a gate with a red brick pathway winding up to the door. Overwhelmed by curiosity, Sebastian proceeded on to the cottage hoping to meet the caretaker.

While stepping closer, a notion grew in Sebastian's mind. Somehow, everything he saw felt strangely familiar to him, as if he knew this place. None of this was like a dream, actually believing he'd been here before. "There will be a crack in the wood on the door next to the doorknob," he whispered. And sure enough, when reaching the cottage entrance, he spied this flaw in the surface, hardly noticeable unless one searched for it.

Closing his eyes before entering the cottage, in his mind, he pictured what it would look like inside. Without knocking, he turned the doorknob, gently pushing the door in. Everything in view was just as he'd imagined it. Blue curtains, disturbed by a draft, flowed in through an open window. A black tea kettle sat on a white antique stove next to a white vintage refrigerator. The replica model of a schooner rested proudly upon a mantle over the fireplace where a sofa and two comfortable chairs were positioned near the hearth. Grinning, he sighed, breathing in the aromas of hickory wood and an apple pie, cooling on the windowsill. Turning to his left, he noticed a cross-stitched picture of the lighthouse hung on the wall. He silently read the embroidered poem at the bottom.

Mariners beware of jagged shores
Hidden by starless nights.
Resist the lure of echoing songs
Tempting sailors to mermaid delights.

Only the true love of your wife and child
Does your heart hear both near and far.
Make haste to the safety of their waiting arms
Guided by the light of the nearest star.

Moving further inside, he walked down a narrow hallway, passing by a bathroom featuring a claw foot tub, before reaching an open door on his right. Inside this bedroom, he saw a desk and chair and an iron bed covered by a patchwork quilt with colors matching the kite outside. Next to the pillow was a book he instantly recognized, *The Wind in the Willows*. Continuing on down the hallway, Sebastian looked through a doorway to the left into another bedroom. A much larger iron bed, covered with a white lace quilt, just barely fit inside with a dresser positioned against the far wall. While standing there, he felt a light scratchy sensation pass against his cheek. This didn't scare him but instead left him strangely comforted

Intending to step inside, Sebastian's steps halted when the door at the hallway's end slightly opened. Cautiously approaching, he placed his hand against the door's white painted surface. Pressing against it, the hinges emitted metallic complaints. Finding the base of the lighthouse tower, Sebastian gazed up, his eyes following a spiraling black circular staircase to the very top. Placing his foot on the first step, his shirt tangled on a metal spindle, tearing and leaving a scratch against his rib cage. "What?" he whispered, only now aware he no longer was wearing a T-shirt, but instead wore a button-down, blue plaid flannel shirt.

The tower remained quiet with exception of his bare feet padding up the metal staircase. The continuous circular climbing had a dizzying effect on Sebastian, causing him to stop a few times to stare out at the clouds through a few small windows. Glancing down offered no respite to the unsteadiness he felt. When he reached the final landing, he noticed a brightness lighting the final few steps.

Emerging out onto an observation platform, his body moved lethargically against forceful gales, rendering him deaf by their intensity. Out over the open water, the seagulls hovered defiantly as the kite quaked in the tempest. A thick veil of fog continued shrouding the distant view, possessively keeping the lighthouse in its clear eye. Sebastian stood still, hypnotized by the never-ending waves impacting upon the shore. Just as he was dragging his eyes away, the silhouette of someone walking down the beach through the ocean spray appeared.

Descending the steps as quickly as he could, Sebastian soon reached the base of the lighthouse tower, discovering an open door swinging in the wind. Once outside, he jogged across the yard to the white picket fence gate. A minute later, he found his way back to the beach, panting for breath, as the walking figure grew smaller in the distance. "Wait! Come back!" Sebastian called out.

Over the thunderous echoing waves, the figure halted, turning back. Glancing down, Sebastian noticed footprints left in the wet sand and followed them while seeing how the figure was now retracing his steps. Anxious to speak to this person, his heart beat faster as the fog drifted onshore, almost as if it were attempting to conceal this person from sight. The figure, clearly a man, stopped just short of stepping into view. Unexplainably, tears soaked Sebastian's eye with one overwhelming thought forcing all others aside. With his pulse racing and swallowing hard, he choked out a word he never thought he would utter, "*Dad.*"

The man fell to his knees, the rolling seafoam washing over his legs. But as his hand reached out, the sight of this man distorted, pixelating as if poor reception on a high definition television. Stepping forward, Sebastian was held back by an invisible barrier as his view of the man deteriorated until an explosive flash of light blinded him.

***

Wave-after-wave of wind-driven rain pounded against the outside of the glass chamber. "No-no-no," Sebastian kept repeating, remembering everything about the lighthouse and the man on the beach. Frantically searching around, he pressed each button on the control panel and pounded his fists against the headphones that had grown silent with their humming.

The door to the glass chamber suddenly opened. Dragged out by his T-shirt, Sebastian's eyes fixed on the drenched face of the black teenage boy standing before him. With the falling rain stinging his face, he couldn't help bursting into tears, pleading to the boy, "Let me go back, please."

"I can't," the teen called out over resounding thunder. He then pulled Sebastian into his arms, comfortingly embracing him. "I wish I could, but I can't."

Pulling away, he turned back to the glass chamber, wanting to climb back inside.

"You'll get electrocuted if you stay out here."

"I need to go back. I need to go back."

"We'll find another way, I promise."

Sebastian watched as the light within the chamber dimmed, realizing that it was losing power. Falling to his knees, he pressed his face against the glass, his breath clouding the surface, reminding him of the fog. "I—need to go—back," he mumbled, feeling crushed, drained of his energy.

The pelting rain against his back lessened as the teen helped him to his feet. Turning around, he looked down, not thinking clearly of anything. Once more, the teen embraced him. "I'll find a way. I promise," he said. Then yielding to defeat, Sebastian trembled, falling apart while the teen ran a soothing hand up and down his back. Forcing Sebastian to look in his face, the teen said, "Come inside. I need to show you something." Not fully understanding, he allowed himself to be led away, glancing back at the now darkened glass chamber before stepping inside the brick building.

***

Staggering out of his private lab in the basement of his house, Lee sat down on the floor, leaning his back against the wall, pulling his knees to his chest. His body shuddered, adrenalized by hearing what he believed was his missing son's voice call out to him. After twelve years, he never would have dared to imagine it being possible.

Alerted that someone had accessed one of his most confidential programs, Lee rushed to his private basement lab, climbing into a glass chamber that had sat dormant for many years. Thinking that his personal database had been hacked, he intended to confront the perpetrator. Yet who he found left him reeling in shock, drawing back every terrible memory of the night his four-year-old son was abducted.

They had gone to Maine with the hopes of disappearing until the authorities could apprehend the person who'd made threats to kidnap his son, Joshua. The lighthouse he'd purchased sight-unseen for his wife, Melinda, was perfectly secluded. He, Melinda, Joshua, and his eight-year-old daughter, Lydia, had been in Maine for only a week before Joshua came down with a high fever. While rushing him to the hospital in Bangor, someone forced their SUV off the road during a storm. Lee could still feel the chill of the river water rushing into the car and remembered watching Melinda's lifeless body floating next to him. As terrible as that was, recalling being trapped in his seat, watching helplessly while someone stole Joshua, proved just as painful to relive.

Forensic experts scouring the crime scene eventually tracked his son's abductor to Boston, but they never found Joshua. The man, a former employee, disgruntled after being terminated, was found dead from an apparent suicide when the police entered his hotel room, taking with him all knowledge of what happened to his son. Disturbingly, the police found a note he held in his hand, with the name *Lydia* written on it. To all, it seemed to confirm the man's intention to kidnap Lee's daughter as well.

Closing his eye, willing all this out of his mind, Lee attempted to focus on facts. Knowing the Daydream chamber's twin sat safe in secured storage underneath One Legacy Place, he reasoned at first that it had somehow malfunctioned. Yet what he saw seemed so vivid until the program abruptly shut down. A nagging suspicion inside him wanted to reject this thought as the complexity of the program included numerous safeguards, where even the theory of malfunction was highly unlikely.

Cyberterrorism next crossed his mind. With all the government contracts Dryden Technologies held, the possibility of hackers gaining access to classified information could not be dismissed. New threats from Eastern Europe and South America were constantly being fought. He'd have to address this with his chief of cybersecurity when he went to his office in the morning.

Standing up, his legs trembling, Lee glanced once more at the Daybreak chamber, wanting in the worst way for Joshua to actually have been trying to reach him. Since he'd been stolen away, the pain never lost any of its intensity and seemed to feel worse each day. With his chest heaving and his heart relentlessly throbbing, Lee slumped back down against the wall. Covering his face with his hands, he burst into tears, grieving once more for his precious missing son.

Chapter Four

"What's your name?"

"Sebastian."

"That's a pretty cool name," the teen responded as the two faced each other. Equal in height, the teen seemed skinnier, having much less hair. One thing they shared was that they both were dripping wet from the rain. Sebastian glanced around the large kitchen they stood in, his stomach muscles contracting with the smell from a plate of brownies on the table.

"Are you hungry?" The teen asked, picking up the plate and holding it out to him.

Hesitating for a moment, Sebastian nodded his head, slowly reaching out for a brownie. "Thanks," he said, avoiding eye contact as he took a bite. It had been a long time since he tasted the richness of chocolate melting in his mouth. "This is really good."

"My name's Scotty," the teen offered, smiling a little. "Um—how old are you?"

"Sixteen."

"Me, too," Scotty confirmed. "Do—you live around here?"

"No." Nervously shifting his weight from one foot the other, Sebastian blurted out, "Are you going to call the police?"

"No. You don't have to worry about that."

"Thanks."

"Would you like some milk?"

Sebastian again nodded his head, watching Scotty walk over to the refrigerator. "You can have another brownie—if you want." Taking the tall cold glass from him, Sebastian reached for another, continuing to avoid direct eye contact. Lightning flashed through the kitchen window, followed by loud thunder.

"Some storm we're having," Scotty mumbled.

"Yeah." After an awkward moment of silence passed, Sebastian summoned enough nerves, asking, "How long was I in that thing?"

"A little over five minutes before the power was drained."

With difficulty swallowing in shock, Sebastian choked out, *"That's—not possible!"*

Scotty smiled before responding, "Follow me."

Climbing a narrow staircase to the second floor, he trailed Scotty down a short hallway to a door at the end. Only after Scotty entered a numeric code onto a keypad did the door open. Once inside the room, Sebastian's eyes grew wide, awed by the numerous computers and the images displayed on each. After uttering, "Wow," he stepped closer to one, squinting at the monitor. Backing away, he retrieved his reading glasses from his backpack.

"You know—they can fix that now with a couple of injections," Scotty commented, noticing Sebastian wearing his glasses. "Nearsightedness, farsightedness, they can even fix color blindness." As his embarrassment must have been obvious, Scotty quickly added, "But—it's okay if you need your glasses. Some people don't like injections."

Wandering over to a dresser, Scotty found a black cut-off T-shirt and a white pair of shorts in the drawers. "Here, you can wear these until your clothes dry."

"Thanks."

After changing, Sebastian sat down on the edge of Scotty's bed, his eyes wandering from one wall to the other, seeing posters of science fiction movies and a picture of Albert Einstein. But the computer monitors were what he really fixed his eyes on. Each one appeared to be running different programs at incredible speeds.

"What is all this?"

"Some might call it a hobby. But—I think of it as a way of someday leaving this place, maybe going to college." Turning to one of the monitors, Scotty revealed, "I've obtained access to practically every database in San Francisco. I can do everything from pulling up video footage shown on surveillance cameras to observing private conversations on social media."

"So…you're a hacker?"

With the slyest of grins, Scotty answered, "I prefer to think of it as enhanced research through alternative means. I've never breached anyone's security *directly*. I simply overstimulate their systems with random data requests until their servers freeze—and I slip in through the back door."

"Back door."

"Yeah, kind of like the exit signs in movie theaters, in this case, a computer programmer's retrieval or escape route."

"I've never heard of anything like that before."

Beaming a smile, Scotty responded, "Most programmers would never admit to the existence of back doors with their programs, but they can be greatly useful if a system is attacked by a cyberterrorist or a computer virus. All they have to do is sneak in the back door of damaged files, salvage the vital information, and exit."

"Sounds easy."

"Sounds easy—but it's not. Practically all software back doors are virtually undetectable—unless you're willing to take the time to look at them." Pointing at one of the computer screens, Scotty challenged, "Take a look at this. I've been searching for the back door to this program for a month—and I still haven't found it."

Sebastian inched his face closer to the screen so his eyes could adjust to the numerous small numbers shown. Almost instantly pointing at the screen, he asked, "What about there in the first column? The sum of that equation is wrong."

Leaning closer with his eyes wide with disbelief, Scotty moved his cursor, highlighting the cell using an Auto Sum to correct the equation. The numbers failed to change, however, the program's back door appeared on the screen. "How—the—heck—did you—do—that?" he mumbled in shock.

Sebastian shrugged his shoulders, not understanding how he discovered it so easy.

Scotty frantically typed a mathematic equation of the screen. "What's the sum of this problem?"

Barely glancing at it, Sebastian quickly answered, "Three thousand two hundred and sixty-eight point two."

After verifying the answer, Scotty sat back in his chair, clearly stunned. "*Unbelievable.* You have the ability to solve complex mathematical equations in your head."

"I've always been good at math."

"*Good*—isn't the word I would use. *Brilliant*—is better."

"I bet lots of people can do that," Sebastian offered, unimpressed by his ability.

"No, trust me—not everybody can."

Feeling uncomfortable at being thought of as brilliant, Sebastian deflected their conversation back to a more comfortable topic. "So what can you tell me about that glass case I was in? You said I was inside for about five minutes—but—it seemed so much longer."

Typing a password on his keyboard, Scotty pulled up an image of the glass chamber on his computer monitor. "What you were inside is called a Daybreak. From all the information I've gathered, there were only two made."

"But—what is it?"

Sitting in a chair next to Scotty's, Sebastian's eyes fixed on the computer screen as a man's facial image appeared. In the back of his mind, he couldn't help but think that there was something familiar about his bearded expression.

"This is Lee Dryden, you know, *Lee—Dryden*, founder of Dryden Technologies." Noticing Sebastian's continued blankness, Scotty commented, "Boy, you must really live out in the fringes. Listen, Lee Dryden created the Daybreak as a gift for his wife. The guy works like over a hundred hours a week. This machine was his way of staying connected with her. Whenever she called him, just wanting to see him, he would step into his Daybreak while she stepped into the twin he built for her. If you think about it, it's kind of a portal in a sense. It was a daydream machine where they could take a break from their hectic days and reconnect through their minds for a few minutes."

"How?"

"At one point, they would have had to visit the same place, sharing detailed memories of it. After that, Lee had both their brains scanned, using advanced technology to imprint their memories into the Daybreak's database. So when they both wanted to reconnect during the day, they would step into their chambers and access the program. And for the next five minutes or longer, in their minds they could be together, wherever that may be, London, Paris, you name it. And it would seem like they were there for hours or even days."

"You make it sound so easy."

Sighing while smiling, Scotty admitted, "It sounds easy, but in reality, it took decades to develop the technology."

Thinking for a moment, Sebastian then asked, "How is it that the machine worked when I was inside?"

"I have no idea," Scotty answered, shaking his head. Staring out while reasoning through this, he continued, "Simply turning on the Daybreak wouldn't be a problem since its solar-powered battery has been baking in the sun for weeks."

"The lightning must have turned it on. I put the headphones on to cover my ears from the thunder. I felt something pinch me. The next thing I knew, I wasn't here anymore, at least not my mind. When I awakened from some sort of trance, I was sitting on a beach near a lighthouse. And—I wasn't alone."

Rubbing his hands over his mouth and jaw, Scotty responded, "The only thing I can think of is that—the program suffered damage from the storm, allowing you access to their memory data. The firewall protecting this information must have failed."

"I—don't think—that it failed."

"Why do you say that?"

Standing up, Sebastian walked over to the window, gazing out at the distant San Francisco night skyline. Releasing a deep sigh, he turned back to Scotty, revealing, "I remembered everything about that place as if I'd been there before. And—"

"And what?"

"I think—the man on the beach—was my dad."

Chapter Five

A sudden knock at the door startled them both. Without invitation, the door swung open with two men standing there. The first, tall, Middle Eastern, and smiling through his bearded face, had long dark hair pulled back in a ponytail. In direct contrast, the other, a clean-shaven, well-groomed, Hispanic stood much shorter at the other's side. "We're home!" The taller man greeted, then looking toward Sebastian. "Who are you?"

"This is my friend, Sebastian," Scotty offered.

"You have a friend?" the taller man, clearly surprised, asked and then received a quick thrust of the shorter man's elbow to his ribcage. "I mean—*welcome*," he corrected himself, wincing through his grin.

"These guys are my dads," Scotty introduced rolling his eyes.

"I'm Xavier and this is Abdul," the shorter man added, both waving at Sebastian.

"Is it okay if Sebastian spends the night?"

"Of *course—provided*—he stays for breakfast. I'm making pancakes," Xavier revealed.

"Thanks, that'd be great," Sebastian responded with a smile.

"Of course, you should make sure your parents are okay with this."

"That won't be a problem," Sebastian responded, looking toward the window as he lied.

"*Ah*, you guys ate the brownies," Abdul complained.

With the door closing, they both overheard Xavier scolding Abdul, "I can make more."

"They're really great," Scotty said, noticeably embarrassed.

"They seem nice."

Deeply sighing, Scotty turned to Sebastian. "Well, aren't you going to ask?"

"Well—okay." Exhaling, he questioned, "Which one named you *Scotty*?"

Bursting with laughter, tears rolled down Scotty's cheeks. Sighing again, he answered, "Both of them. They're big science fiction geeks. They offered me the name of their favorite character from *Star Trek. Actually*—the question I thought you were going to ask was—if I'm gay, too."

"Well—I assumed that—by the picture of Einstein on your wall," Sebastian dryly answered, sending Scotty into another fit of laughter.

Composing himself again, Scotty revealed, "I am—gay. That's the reason they were allowed to adopt me. It's been two of the best years of my life being with them." Awkwardly, he then asked, "Does this bother you?"

"To be honest—I'm disappointed—there's no more brownies," continuing to make light of everything. Smiling, he seriously responded, "No, it doesn't bother me. I'm—*not*. Does that bother you?"

"No," Scotty answered, grinning. Turning his attention back to his closest laptop computer, he pulled up another image of the Daybreak chamber.

"What are you looking for?" Sebastian asked, moving his chair closer.

"Crumbs."

"*Crumbs*?"

Glancing back at Sebastian, Scotty explained, "When I first pulled this up tonight, I spied something missing from when I researched this yesterday. I think—someone might have been alerted that either I had accessed this database—or was alerted earlier tonight when you were inside the Daybreak. Part of the program has definitely been deleted."

"So the information is gone," Sebastian commented.

"Not—necessarily. With certain current software, when something is deleted—it's gone forever. Dryden Technologies, however, uses software deletion protocols which delay deletion for twenty-four hours, in the event that data is being deleted by accident, giving programmers a chance to rethink their changes or correct errors before it's too late. They use encryption on information being discarded, completely indecipherable, looking like random symbols. But to access this—we need to find the crumb that was left.

"What does a crumb look like?"

"Could be an awkwardly placed asterisk, among other things."

"What about the smiley-face symbol in the bottom left-hand corner?"

"It wouldn't be that obvious. Look." Moving his cursor to the point Sebastian observed, Scotty right clicked on it. Encrypted information instantly appeared across the screen. "Are you kidding me? No way," Scotty exclaimed. Sighing, he added, "But—it will take a few hours for my system to decode it." Looking to Sebastian, he remarked, "You look tired. You should go to sleep. Take the bed. I'll sleep on the floor." Anticipating his refusal, Scotty pointed at the bed, "Go—to sleep."

"What about you?"

"I'm going to stay up a little while longer. There's something I need to do."

***

Once sure Sebastian had fallen asleep, Scotty began searching on his laptop through websites for missing children. From the moment they met, he knew Sebastian was a runaway and wanted nothing more than to help him find his way off the streets. Remembering his own experiences with running away, he couldn't let someone else go through what he had. Yet site after site yielded no traces of his new friend. Running his hands across his head in frustration, Scotty thought for a moment before deciding to alter his investigation.

Connecting with San Francisco's Family Services database, he found ease in maneuvering around their protection programs, enabling him to search through hundreds of photographed children placed in foster care and group homes. Roughly an hour later, having viewed far too many pictures of kids less fortunate than him, Scotty finally came across Sebastian's picture. And with the right-click of his cursor, his friend's file appeared on the screen.

Dating back to the age of four, he'd been passed around numerous foster homes stretching from Essex, New Hampshire, to here in San Francisco almost five years ago. With little details offered as to why, the only thing certain was that the system had failed in providing him with a safe, loving home.

Continuing with his research, Scotty's jaw dropped when Sebastian's medical records appeared. His eyes grew teary, moving through numerous images showing bruised skin, black eyes, and several x-rays of broken bones. In thinking back to the abuse he suffered at the hands of his drug-addicted foster parents, he silently promised to never let that happen to Sebastian again.

When skimming the last health record's entry, dated three months ago, Scotty's eyes grew large, bewildered in trying to comprehend what he read. Rereading it several times, his heart sank deeper and deeper. Quickly exiting Sebastian's files, he conducted another search for needed information, feeling devastated when finding the results. Swallowing hard, he brushed aside his tears, attempting to control his rapid breathing.

"Think—think—think," he repeated, lightly pounding his fist against his head. For the longest time, he remained lost in his thoughts until a distant flash of lightning through his window jarred him away from his trance. Suddenly, in his mind, the sliver of an answer appeared.

While in the Daybreak, Sebastian thought he'd seen his father, highly impossible. Yet this comment brought Scotty back to the information listed with Family Services. Sebastian's records started when he was four-years-old. No one's history excludes the first four years of their life. So what happened to him before his first foster home in New Hampshire? What about his parents?

Accessing public records for New Hampshire, he scoured obituaries listing the deceased in and around Essex prior to the official date listed on Sebastian's information. In the month's leading up to that date, not one article described a couple who had died, leaving behind a four-year-old son. With his frustration growing, Scotty continued skimming through articles until a small headline appeared on the screen, *The Desperate Search for a Missing Child Comes to New Hampshire.* Needing just to read the first paragraph, something only moments before, seeming impossible, now held a mind-boggling probability.

Police Chief, Cyrus Bellingham confirmed today that the search for missing four-year-old Joshua Dryden has expanded to the city of Essex. Little Joshua was abducted near Bangor, Maine one week ago after a car accident. While authorities are withholding certain details, citizens are urged to contact police should they have information as to the boy's whereabouts.

"Dear God, are you Joshua Dryden?" Scotty whispered.

Intending to conduct a web search for Joshua Dryden's birth certificate, he was halted by an incoming email. Accessing his inbox, Scotty nearly stopped breathing while reading the message.

From: Dryden One:
We need to talk, face-to-face. Meet me tomorrow night at 8 pm on the upper observation floor at One Legacy Place. Come alone. Everything you wish to know will be revealed.
LD

Chapter Six

Sebastian woke more tired than he'd ever felt. At least the nightmare left him alone for one night. Glancing at the tremor gripping his hand, he brushed it off as nerves although he didn't feel anxious. If anything, for the first time in recent memory, he felt safe.

Looking across the room, he grinned, seeing Scotty asleep with his head resting next to his laptop. He hadn't meant to startle him, but when he sat up in bed, Scotty instantly woke, rubbing his eyes.

"Good morning. How'd you sleep?" he asked in a groggy, sleep laden voice.

"Fine, I guess," Sebastian answered, stretching his arms over his head.

They both turned toward the door, alerted by a soft knock. "Breakfast is ready, boys," they heard Abdul say.

Before reaching the kitchen door, Sebastian breathed in the pleasant aromas of coffee and bacon. His stomach muscles contracted enough to cause Scotty to chuckle. Stepping into the kitchen, Sebastian watched Xavier busy stirring a pan of scrambled eggs and couldn't help but smile at the words printed on Abdul's white tank top, *Stressed for Success*. His bulging muscular frame seemed even more formidable than when he first met him. Xavier, in contrast, was geek-chic from head to toe, dressed in a button-down blue dress shirt under a black cardigan and plaid trousers.

"If you mention those brownies again, I will beat you," Xavier scolded over his shoulder.

"Promise," Abdul jokingly responded, then receiving the blunt impact of a spatula at the back of his head.

"Good morning, boys. Pancakes will be ready in a minute," Xavier said, again over his shoulder. Abdul poured orange juice for all of them as they sat down. "Dig in," Xavier invited.

With his hunger ravenous, Sebastian made sure to slowly devour his heaping breakfast. As he ate, he noticed how Scotty was distracted.

"Is the annual summer office party tonight?"

"Yes. Why would you ask about that?" Abdul questioned, sipping his coffee.

"You hate the summer office party. You refused to go last year," Xavier chimed in.

"Well—I'd like to go this year—and take Sebastian with us, if that's okay."

Abdul, Xavier, and Sebastian stopped eating, watching Scotty.

"Who are you—and what have you done with Scotty?" Abdul dryly demanded.

"I just thought—it might be nice—for Sebastian to see One Legacy Place, that's all," Scotty responded, glancing at each one.

Crookedly smiling, Abdul asked, "What are you after? What are you attempting to access?"

"You realize we could be fired if you get caught?" Xavier reprimanded Scotty.

Abdul interrupted, holding up his hand to Xavier. "Let him speak."

Sebastian looked to Scotty as his friend asked, "What can you tell me about the Daybreak chamber outside?"

With a knowing grin, Abdul answered, "So you're trying to get that thing to work? The Daybreak happens to be one of Lee Dryden's most technologically sophisticated toys—and is completely beyond your grasp. Only he can access the information stored in it."

"What's it doing here?" Sebastian blurted out.

"It was in storage at One Legacy Place until a few weeks ago when some housecleaning was done in the storage units. They marked it as trash and it was hauled away. It came to us because we have the nearest dump site," Abdul replied.

"Why would Lee Dryden throw something so valuable away?" Scotty asked.

"Possibly—he wanted to rid himself of painful memories it invoked? After all, he developed it for his wife. After she died, he had it removed. Maybe—he found the will to let it—and her go," Abdul speculated.

"And—maybe—it wasn't him who got rid of it," Xavier interjected. All three stared at him until he added, "The transfer invoice for it came across my desk with the initials *L* and *D*. Lee Dryden isn't the only one in the executive suites with those initials."

"Who else?" Sebastian asked.

"His current wife, Lexia Dryden, and his daughter, Lydia Dryden," Xavier replied.

"Lydia, the ice princess," Scotty added.

"*Ice princess*?"

"You'll see," Abdul, Xavier, and Scotty said in unison.

"Go on. You know you want to," Abdul encouraged Xavier, grinning at him.

Leaning in, as if wanting to quietly tell a secret, corporate gossip spilled from Xavier's lips. "Rumor has it that Lee Dryden wants to retire."

"How old is he?" Sebastian wondered.

"Forty-five. Of course, for billionaires, age doesn't matter for retirement. Anyway, word is that behind the scenes—there's a power struggle between Lydia and her mother as to who should take over. Neither wants the other to gain control. The board of directors believes that Lydia, at age twenty, is too young to lead the company. As for her mother, Senator Lexia Dryden's term in Washington doesn't expire for another two years, leaving her unable to assume power if Lee should step down before then. Boys, this should be quite an evening at One Legacy Place."

Sighing, Abdul sarcastically commented, "Of course it will, standing there, basking in the disdainful, condescending, glances of the evil queen and the devious ice princess. Someone pinch me."

***

The scorching afternoon sunlight heated the air in Sebastian's utility room, forcing him to seek refuge outside under a partially shaded spot with the full view of the San Francisco skyline. Stray clouds passing overhead reflected their impressive images off the windows of several glass towers with white trams gliding along their silvery rails above boulevards dotted with speeding driverless electric cars.

Still tired from what he guessed must not have been a restful sleep during the night, he attempted to nap for a while in a hammock he'd strung. A slight noise, however, caused him to open his eyes, stiffly leaning up where he could see Scotty step closer.

"You followed me here?"

"No, well—not really. I tracked you. Before you left I hide an old cell phone in the bottom of your backpack and used an app on my Smartphone to locate your position," Scotty shamefully confessed.

"Why?"

Stammering a bit, Scotty responded, "I don't want you to be angry with me. It's just, —well—I—don't have many friends, as you might have guessed. And—I didn't want you to go. Being that it's summer, I don't see any of my high school classmates, not that any of them hang out with me. Most of the guys in my class play sports or chase girls. They don't get my obsession with computers and technology. Maybe you don't either. But—you seemed interested, more than anyone else before." Lowering his head, Scotty finished, "Sometimes—it gets pretty lonely. I told you my dads both work a lot at Dryden. They usually get home late. Most days there's just no one to talk to."

"I understand," Sebastian offered.

Sighing, Scotty mumbled, "I'm sorry. I should go."

"Stay. It's okay. I'd like some company."

"Are you sure?"

"Yeah, it's okay."

Smiling now, Scotty dragged his backpack off. "I brought you something," he said, digging inside. Pulling out a book, he handed it to Sebastian. "I'm not sure if you've read this. It's called *Brave New World*."

"No, I haven't," Sebastian responded, sitting up and paging through it. "I saw it there—but I didn't have enough room in my backpack to take it with me."

"You're smart to read actual books. You know the government monitors electronic book purchases, keeping an eye on people who read radical doctrines and stuff they find obscene. They can access anyone's electronic library, all your personal information."

"Why am I not surprised by that?" Sebastian said matter-of-fact. While scanning the pages, tremors in his left hand forced him to close the book. He noticed Scotty staring at this. "My hands—shake—when I get tired," he self-consciously revealed.

"I should let you get some sleep."

"No. Stay. I'm stiff. I just need to get up and move around." Glancing over against the wall, he spied his basketball. "I have a rim over there. Do you want to shoot some hoops?"

"Sure!"

"Maybe we could play horse?"

Scotty grinned. "How 'bout Daybreak," he countered.

"Sounds good," Sebastian agreed, smiling.

During their game, with Scotty losing miserably, Sebastian held the ball, his curiosity forcing him to ask, "What's tonight going to be like?"

"Well—the party is a complete geek fest, with mostly computer programmers from the various divisions intermingling. The food is okay, nothing special. They usually have a band playing retro techno pop, not unexpected for the crowd."

"And the Dryden's will be there?"

"Yeah, kind of."

"What do you mean?"

Leaning against the wall, Scotty answered, "Lee Dryden seldom talks to anyone—but you see him walking around, mostly staring out the window. It's pretty obvious he doesn't want to be there. His wife will give a welcome speech. But trust me, you won't feel very welcome after hearing it. And as for Lydia, there's something really *disturbing*—about her."

Sebastian asked, "*Disturbing*?" while leaning his own back against the wall.

"First of all, she's a genius, just like you."

"I'm no genius."

"Yes, you are. Anyway, by the age of six, she was designing complex algorithms while solving mathematical equations that would take experts years to solve. Her IQ is off the charts."

"So, she's a genius. Why does that make her disturbing?"

"Her genius is the most normal part about her. It's everything else that makes her disturbing. When she talks to you, it's as if you're being interrogated, like she's gathering as much information about you as possible. But—she will never answer a question asked to her. She just smiles and walks away. And Lydia is also the vainest person I've ever met. She wears a tiara, probably worth a fortune, that has a computer chip embedded into it. When she touches the biggest diamond, a virtual computer screen appears in front of her eyes so she can track how she's trending on social media."

"She sounds really full of herself."

Resting his head back against the wall, Scotty turned away, looking out toward downtown San Francisco. "The worst thing of all is her eyes. They're the most lifeless, fake eyes I've ever seen."

"I can't wait to meet her," Sebastian responded, completely sure he *didn't* want to.

"Stay close to me and my dads. Maybe you'll get lucky and she won't notice you."

Looking down at his bare feet, torn blue jeans and old white T-shirt, Sebastian sarcastically remarked, "I'm sure she won't notice me."

Slightly laughing, Scotty urged, "Come back to my place. I've got some clothes that should fit you. We'll leave for the party from there."

"Well—if the party is gonna be anything like you said, I should probably wear a plaid suit and sweater vest," Sebastian commented, causing Scotty to laugh deeper. But smiling on the outside, he couldn't help but feel nervous about going. It was more than just knowing he didn't belong among those people. Something nagging in the back of his mind, warnings he couldn't understand, urged him to stay away from there, but it was too late to turn back.

Chapter Seven

"Allow me to be perfectly clear. Corduroy is not making a fashion comeback, not now and not ever," Xavier mumbled under his breath to Abdul.

Puffing his massive chest out as he ran his hands down his brown corduroy jacket, Abdul sighed contently. "My suit will make a statement tonight," he proudly commented.

Xavier's eyes bulged out of their sockets as he turned to Abdul, noticeably dismayed by this remark. "And—just what kind of statement does a walking carpet make?"

"It is geek-chic, much like your navy blue plaid suit," Abdul uttered with satisfaction.

"It is an *unforgivable* fashion crime," Xavier countered.

Both Sebastian and Scotty refrained from offering their thoughts on Abdul's suit. In truth, it was tailored to perfection over his muscular frame, but the color left him resembling a walking forest. Checking his own reflection on a chrome strip at the tram station, Sebastian kind of liked the collarless white button-down linen shirt and black dress pants Scotty had loaned him. He'd also given him a pair of black converse sneakers to use, making the outfit youthful and casual. Scotty wore a silky black dress shirt, white sneakers, and gray pants. Of all four of them, he appeared the least comfortable dressed up and far more nervous than Sebastian felt.

"Are you okay? You look like you're about to pass out."

"I'm fine. I just have a few things on my mind," Scotty answered, grinning unconvincingly. Glancing down, he pointed at Sebastian's hand, gripped once more by a tremor. "How 'bout you?"

Exhaling his nerves, Sebastian shrugged his shoulders without saying a word.

The flickering of the overhead lights drew their attention up as did the distant sound of rolling thunder. Looking around in confusion, Sebastian wondered where the storm was, as the early evening sky shone with a vivid molasses color, not a cloud in sight. An anxious glance shared by Abdul and Xavier did not go unnoticed by him.

With the polished white tram reaching the platform, all four edged forward, ready to step inside. When the doors parted, Abdul took the lead, with Xavier and Scotty quickly following. Sebastian hesitated for a moment before stepping onto the tram, his pulse beginning to race. Gliding smoothly away from the platform, he barely felt the motion under his feet as the only evidence they were moving was the passing view of the city.

Traveling through the lower class district, Sebastian blankly stared out at the familiarity through the window. Yet, he couldn't help, what with seeing two police vehicles traveling at high-speed toward a nearby college campus, in thinking that something was off. Scuffles between protesting students and authorities in San Francisco had been a common occurrence for almost a century. Over the last few years, however, ordinary citizens were adding their voices to the demonstrations, objecting to increasing government censorship and limits on civil liberties.

As their tram rounded a corner, heading toward the downtown district, it abruptly came to a halt, jarring everyone inside. The overhead lights quickly dimmed, plunging the inside of the tram into darkness. Sebastian's heart beat faster as his eyes grew large, watching the scene unfolding on the street below the tram rails. Hundreds of protestors and policemen, marching together, halted only a short distance away from lines, four rows deep, of what appeared to be soldiers. "Who are they?" Sebastian wondered aloud.

Quietly, Abdul revealed, "This morning—the mayor of San Francisco, with the blessing of the city council, and Senator Lexia Dryden terminated the entire police force in favor of a private security force funded by numerous corporations. Hundreds of officers lost their jobs in this cost-saving effort by the city, each one being replaced by highly trained paramilitary officers. Many are angry that they had no voice in this change—and just as many are concerned that the new officers may hold extreme dispositions toward those who break the law and could potentially infringe upon the privacy rights of citizens. All is seen as a thinly veiled marriage between the government and the corporate sectors, shifting us further toward totalitarianism."

The bellowing of the crowd must have been deafening, for they could hear some noise through the tram windows that were designed to be soundproof. From the corner of his eye, Sebastian watched Xavier cover his mouth in dismay with one hand as he reached out for Abdul with his other hand. Turning to Scotty, he saw his friend's eyes completely transfixed on the crowd.

Blinding glares from floodlights burst, catching the protesters and policemen off guard, with many shielding their eyes and retreating from where they stood. The new security guards then began taunting the mob, waving their batons and hands in the air.

Looking to Abdul, Sebastian uttered in disbelief, "They are trying to provoke the protestors. Am I seeing this right?"

"Yes," Abdul answered, swallowing hard as he placed his hand on Sebastian's shoulder to calm him.

Glancing down again, Sebastian's held his breath when the security guards fired water cannons at the protesters, sending many people to their knees or staggering away. His heart stopped when a barrage of gunfire exploded upon the crowd, the bodies of many dropping instantly. Placing his palms against the glass, Sebastian watched in horror as many of the people running away were gunned down. And then a chill ran down his spine when his eyes locked on a security guard who stood staring back, threateningly pointing his baton up at him.

The overhead flickering of the lights preceded the forceful forward jerking motion of the tram, quickly leaving the carnage behind. With his last glimpse being of the street stained red with blood, Sebastian heard Abdul's urging, "Please, all of you. Do not speak of what you just watched to anyone. Should the authorities discover the presence of witnesses to this unprovoked attack by the police on the demonstrators, the consequences could be severe."

Not revealing that an officer had stared him down, Sebastian fought to release his words, "So—they-get-away-with-it."

"Yes," Abdul gravely whispered.

***

With his thoughts still distracted by the carnage he witnessed a short while ago, Sebastian was unable to focus on San Francisco's central district until Scotty pointed out all the grandeur through the tram windows upon their arrival. Boulevards and walkways as white and pristine as new fallen snow contrasted against vivid green belts featuring small trees and well-manicured plants and bushes. Colorful murals and modern sculptures held prominence from one courtyard to the next. And rising from this impressive landscape were monolithic steel and glass towers, reflecting the brilliant late-afternoon reddish sky.

"They look like they're bleeding," he faintly murmured to himself, his growing anxiety matching his speeding pulse. Tapping Scotty's arm, he asked, "Which building is One Legacy Place?"

"The smaller white one in the center. Decades ago, it was called the Transamerica Pyramid, before Dryden Technologies bought the building and renamed it."

Stepping off the tram, Sebastian's eyes were drawn away from the architecture to watching the people. Men and women of every race passed by, each impeccably dressed. A few older people appeared in the crowd every so often, but mostly the people seemed to be in their thirties and forties. "Notice anything about them?" Scotty quietly asked.

"What should I have noticed?" Sebastian wearily replied back.

"Not one of them is overweight."

Searching, Sebastian soon realized that Scotty was right. "I don't understand."

"To control health costs, each of the companies here in the Center District enacted employee regulations about a person's weight. If your Body Mass Index does not meet regulations, they can fire you as a health risk."

"*Unbelievable*."

Under his breath, Scotty added, "Senator Dryden, Lee's wife, is spearheading an effort in Congress to have the same rules apply for federal employees."

"Isn't that like a form of discrimination? Some can't help it. A lot of people could lose their jobs."

"Welcome to the year 2035, my friend," Scotty mumbled.

***

Following Scotty and his dads through the set of main doors of One Legacy Place, Sebastian stopped dead in his tracks, awed by the enormity of just the lobby. Fountains illuminated by colorful LED lights were positioned at opposite ends and seemingly comfortable couches and chairs were set off in various areas. The polished marble floors and massive modern art sculptures and paintings added to the opulence.

Catching up with Scotty and his dads, they all stood waiting for their turn before a bank of stainless-steel elevators to be taken to the highest levels of the tower. His hand rubbed across his chest, hoping to calm his pounding heart as his other hand spasmed at his side. Swallowing hard, he was overwhelmed by the thought of backing away and leaving. And then the doors to the elevator silently opened. Feeling dizzy, he staggered a step but was caught by Abdul. "Are you all right? You look pale," he commented.

"I've—never been on—an elevator," Sebastian truthfully revealed, not fully understanding the fears he had no words for.

Smiling, Abdul followed him into the elevator, placing both hands on Sebastian's shoulders to steady him. "It's completely safe in here. I promise." Abdul reassured him as Xavier pressed the button for the observation floor. Feeling slightly weightless for a moment, he released the breath he had been holding as the elevator began its ascent. Turning to Scotty, Abdul reminded him, "You won't have any cell phone service until we leave. For security purposes, One Legacy Place is a dead zone."

Glancing cautiously around at the inner frosted glass panes lining the elevator's interior, he breathed in sterile air tainted with a slight fragrance from the carpeted flooring. To his left, images of consumers and employees appeared on a floor-to-ceiling screen, accompanied by a synthetic voice extolling Dryden Technologies achievements and world standing. To his ears, however, it sounded mostly like someone babbling on about nothing important.

Feeling another moment of weightlessness as the elevator came to a halt, Sebastian's body shuddered, jumping back with fear when a high-pitched ring preceded the opening of the elevator doors.

Chapter Eight

"Which one is Lexia Dryden?" Sebastian whispered, following Scotty and his dads through the crowd. In truth, the party proved exactly how Scotty described it would be, easily deciphering the computer programmers from corporate executives by how they were dressed and how the groups kept from intermingling. The music, definitely techno pop, found some awkwardly dancing to it as others ridiculously bobbed their heads to the rhythm. Tables providing a variety of food and sparkling beverages lined the nearest wall with the programmers scavenging under disdainful glances from several executives.

"Over there, in the corner. The stunning black woman wearing the emerald-colored dress—vainly admiring her reflection in the window," Abdul answered Sebastian, motioning his head in her direction. Carefully looking over, not wanting to get caught staring, Sebastian watched her. Slender and tall, Lexia Dryden's appearance suggested a complete control of the roomful of men surrounding her. Each approaching man either bowed his head or hesitated before talking to her, nervous as they spoke. Her expression never altered from that of uninterested bystander, responding in one or two word answers.

Silently wondering for a moment why Lee Dryden had married her, under his breath Xavier unleashed his gift of gossip, revealing the answer to Sebastian's unspoken question. "Lee Dryden met her at the 2012 London Olympic Games. She was competing as a distance runner from Somalia. They met through mutual friends and fell madly in love. He found out about her being pregnant with

Lydia after their affair ended. A few years later, Lee married Melinda. And about a year after Melinda's death—Lexia and Lee got back together and were married a few months later."

Under his breath, Abdul mumbled to Scotty, "Whatever you're planning to do, you should do it soon. The party only lasts a couple of hours." Nodding his head, Scotty pulled Sebastian away from his dads, toward the windows.

"Listen, it's 7:30, I need to sneak away at 8 pm. You can't follow me. I need to do this on my own," Scotty whispered.

Nodding his head, Sebastian understood. Turning toward the windows, he noticed the reflection of a man closely staring at them. Mumbling under his breath, he asked, "Scotty, look at our reflection. Who is that watching us?"

Glancing at their reflection, Scotty answered, "Gideon Temple. He's Lee Dryden's executive director and chief security administrator, kind of his number two guy."

"Do you think he knows you've been accessing Dryden files?"

"I don't know. I don't think so—but I can't be sure." Scotty seemed anxious. "We have company. The ice princess is coming."

With both slowly turning away from the outside view, Lydia Dryden's approach halted as she stopped in front of them. Partly understanding why Scotty referred to her as the 'ice princess', Sebastian found himself confused by how unexpected she looked. Both slender and tall like her mother, her smooth ebony-colored skin dramatically contrasted to her bleach-white, long, straight hair and form-fitting white cocktail dress. Wearing white stiletto heels, she towered over them both. Drawn to her eyes with their long, spiked lashes and white eyeshadow, Sebastian felt vulnerable and intimidated by her stare. Smiling at them both, with her soft voice lacking any natural lilt, she asked, "Who is your friend, Scotty?"

Stammering and clearing his throat, he responded, "This is Sebastian."

Now under her direct glare, she continued, "Welcome to our party, Sebastian. We should talk alone later, get to know each other."

Gathering his courage, he boldly asked, "What do you want to know about me?" Grinning as if possibly interpreting his question as a challenge, Lydia wandered away without answering.

"When you said 'ice princess', she wasn't what I thought of."

"Be careful," Scotty warned. "Don't go anywhere alone with her. Don't trust her."

"I won't."

The ringing of a chime drew everyone's attention to the center of the room where Lexia Dryden stood, nodding her head to a few people near her. "Good evening," her noticeably deep accented, smoky voice offered. "Welcome to Dryden Technologies annual summer gala, as usual, an impressive gathering of our brightest minds, visionaries— each one of you." Taking a step, her expression altered to a sympathetic frown. "Although—our vision as the ultimate leader of world technology—has become *somewhat—* opaque." Sighing, she continued, "The formidable achievements of our competitors threaten to tarnish our impeccable standing at the forefront of the technology industry. With the competitive progress made by others, as well as the influx of low-quality imports from the Far East and South America, our task in maintaining a significant profit—has grown precarious."

Abdul slyly expressed a sarcastic smile to Sebastian and Scotty as she spoke further. "If I may speak—from the vantage point of a potential consumer, the recent trade conference in Tokyo—was rather—*lackluster*—with regards to our coming innovations. Therefore, with the agreement and urging of the board of directors, our current software development projects are hereby suspended." Halting her words due to audible gasps from many, Lexia continued, "A revamped line-up of products and programs must be presented to the board in seven days."

The deafening silence following these words was met with a smile adorning her face. "Please enjoy the cuisine—and thank you for your continuing dedication to Dryden Technologies." Gideon Temple rapidly approached her, whispering in her ear after addressing those gathered. Frantically spying around, it seemed to Sebastian that she was searching the crowd for someone. Worrying that she might be trying to find Scotty, he looked to the left and found himself standing there alone. Scotty had disappeared.

***

Walking cautiously around the observation level overlooking the party below, Scotty approached Lee Dryden. Noticing how he seemed to be blankly staring off, he cleared his throat alerting him to his presence. Glancing toward Scotty, a grin burst across his lightly bearded face. "Of *course*! Why did I bother hiring the brightest minds in computer protection—with not one of them being able to stop a teenage boy from hacking into our most secured data? Don't worry, Scotty. I won't tell your dads. To be honest I really couldn't care less." Placing his index finger to his lips, Lee then asked, "The only thing I want to know is how—were you able to access the stored data in my Daybreak machine? You shouldn't have been able to do that. Other than me, the only people who could do that were—"

"Your wife—and son," Scotty interrupted.

Closing his eyes for a moment, as if Scotty had injured him with his words, Lee responded, "Yes."

Stepping next to Lee and glancing down at the party, Scotty confessed, "I wasn't the one who accessed the information in your Daybreak machine. "Joshua did, or rather *Sebastian*, as he calls himself."

Trembling, overwhelmed with emotion, his chest heaved under his white V-neck T-shirt, Lee covered his mouth with his hands.

"Maybe it's just a coincidence. Maybe the data was damaged enough to allow someone to access it. *Maybe*— Sebastian isn't your son," Scotty suggested.

Swallowing hard, Lee uttered, "Melinda—wanted to name him Sebastian—but—I insisted on Joshua—with Sebastian as his middle name." Staring now at Scotty, Lee revealed, "The program is flawless. It can't be damaged or hacked or corrupted. Only *three* people could access the data, Me, Melinda, and—"

"Your son."

"Yes," Lee breathlessly confirmed. "We didn't know it at the time, but when Melinda's brain waves were scanned, she was pregnant with him. His brain waves were scanned too."

Motioning with his head toward the party, Scotty whispered, "He's here, your son is down there."

"*Where!*" Lee uttered, nearly leaping over the edge, his eyes frantically searching the crowd.

Pointing down, Scotty spotted Sebastian standing next to the furthest window. "He's over there, across the room." Following his hand, Lee's eyes exploded, seeing his son for the first time in twelve years. Scotty watched as tears escaped from the corner of Lee's eyes as he exhaled deeply. The tears streaming down his face intensified with Scotty's next revelation. "There's something you need to know, something—I don't think he even knows. According to his medical records, he's in the early stages of Parkinson's disease." Lee's legs appeared to grow weak as he struggled to remain standing. "I thought people couldn't get that anymore."

Wiping his tears away, Lee responded, "Only—if they were given the vaccine at the right time—before any symptoms appeared."

"Will—the vaccine work if given to him now?"

"No, it's too late. I can't stop it—but—I could delay it from getting worse."

"How?"

Composing himself, Lee responded, "Daybreak. If I can get him to the other machine, we can access the program and slow the symptoms from getting worse. It won't cure him, but—maybe the effects of Parkinson's will be diminished to the point where it acts dormant."

"But isn't your machine just an illusion?" Scotty argued.

"I'm not a magician with a vanishing cabinet trying to pull off some kind of parlor trick," Lee snapped.

Scotty offered, "Only our minds have access to the program. Our physical bodies remain here in the real world."

"Remember old science fiction movies about space travel—where the astronaut's bodies were placed into a deep sleep, preserving them? That's what happens in the Daybreak, only in reverse. An hour *there*—is only a minute *here*," Lee answered. "My machine took old science fiction—and turned it into science fact. By slowing his vital signs down in such a way, the Daybreak can delay the natural progression of the disease."

Thinking this through, Scotty confirmed, "So—by having your son go into this chamber, his physical body would be placed in some sort of suspended hibernation state—with his mind experiencing a fantasy world." Angrily he then added, "*Why not*—just find some old psychotropic drugs and have him *trip out* like they did a long time ago."

Looking down at Sebastian, Lee frustratingly whispered, "That's all I have. It's the only way I can be with him."

"It's not living," Scotty whispered back. "It's hiding."

Swallowing deep, Lee revealed, "That's *exactly* what we need to do, him and I. Everything is falling apart around me—all beyond my control. Each time I turn around, I'm confronted with hidden agendas and lies. It's only going to get worse. Please, I'm begging you to understand this. I failed my son once—and look what happened. The Daybreak is the only place I know of where I can take him and care for him, and keep him safe. Even if it's just a few minutes here, maybe it could be a lifetime there."

Sighing out his own frustration, Scotty asked, "How long could both of you stay in there?"

Running his hands over his face and through his hair, Lee responded, "Any duration of time here in the real world can be selected simply by programming the internal clock for however long desired. Physically, being placed in hibernation, I'm not sure. Days, weeks, months, I don't know. For extended use, such as I'm suggesting, the Daybreak has the ability to monitor vital signs and will suspend the program if it detects any sort of health crisis for either of us."

"Won't it detect Sebastian's Parkinson's disease?"

"Yes, it will. I should be able to impute this information into the database so that he can access the program." Stepping closer to him, Lee added, "I understand your point of view on all this. And maybe is *does* sound foolish for the fraction of time I'm asking for. But—I *need* this time with him. I'm begging you. Please help me."

"How very touching. If only—you could get to your machine?" Lexia Dryden commented, stepping out of the shadows, accompanied by Gideon Temple. Footsteps from the opposite direction alerted the four of them to someone else approaching.

"What have we here? Are you thinking of going away, Daddy?" Lydia asked, her grin as fake as Scotty always remembered. "Are you going to take my brother with you? That is him down there, the boy in the white shirt, isn't he?" Stepping between her father and mother, Lydia confessed, "I should have killed him myself while I had the chance. I hired the man you terminated for corporate spying to do the job—but he was weak and greedy."

"I know," Lee admitted. "He contacted me after the accident, telling me how my eight-year-old daughter wanted him to murder her brother, my son. He sent me your text messages and confirmation of money you deposited in his bank account. He wanted another million to reveal where he'd taken your brother—and I would have paid it and a whole lot more." Turning toward Lexia, he continued, "But my greedy, jealous ex-girlfriend, your beautiful mother, and now my devoted wife, paid to have that man killed, taking with him to his grave where he'd hidden my son. I had hoped, by keeping you both close, that over time one of you would have slipped up—letting me find out where Joshua was."

Scotty stood paralyzed, listening to Lee Dryden expose his wife and daughter's treachery. Lexia offered no emotions after hearing her husband uncover her deceit. Looking at Scotty, Lee added, "I found out my wife's secret—by following the crumbs. You know what I'm talking about." Scotty slowly shook his head in understanding. His heart then stopped when Lydia withdrew a small gun from her white handbag, pointing it at her father while strolling over to the glass railing.

"How did you get a handgun? Current laws forbid personal firearms in the city," Scotty noted. Lydia, of course, ignored the question.

"Now, Lydia, dearest. Let's not be hasty," Lexia calmly interjected. "We need your father's access code—in order to take control of Dryden Technologies. Unfortunately, Gideon has failed to secure this through his access to the corporate database."

"I *told*—you, it was impossible," Gideon growled to Lexia.

Lydia smirked, waving the gun around as if a toy before pointing it down at Sebastian.

"Why don't you just ask for it?" Lee calmly asked, glancing at Scotty rather than his wife and daughter. Not waiting for either to respond, he casually looked around and then said, "Voice access Dryden Legacy database."

"Password authorization required," a monotone male voice spoke out from an overhead speaker. Gideon searched around for the source of the voice as Lexia and Lydia stood still without reacting.

"January 6, 2019."

"Joshua's birthday," Lydia confirmed.

"Password authorization verified," the monotone male voice confirmed.

"Initiate Nightfall," Lee said, looking directly at his wife who then backed slowly away, appearing slightly startled.

Glancing with confusion to her father, Lydia lowered her weapon. Unexpectedly, Gideon lunged forward at Lydia, grabbing hold of her gun, with the two struggling to take it from each other. Swinging her around, the gun fired as it pointed up at her face, sending her staggering back. Grasping at Gideon's jacket, she held on to him as they both smashed through the glass, falling over the balcony and landing below in the room's center. An eruption of yelling and screaming echoed as people rushed out of the way.

Stepping up to the gaping hole in the splintered glass, Scotty looked down. Covering his mouth, he gazed upon Gideon's lifeless body and the shattered remains of Lydia, her face broken, revealing the robotic mechanisms sparking inside her head.

Chapter Nine

Watching Lydia and Gideon fall off the balcony, Sebastian stepped backward in fear, pressing up against the window. In the ensuing chaos, watching people running in each direction, he had no idea where his friend Scotty went as he searched for him. Knocked to the side by two frightened programmers, strong arms pulled Sebastian to his feet. "This way," Abdul called over the loud voices. Pushing through those gathered near the elevators, he clung to Abdul who led him toward an unmarked gray metal door behind the staircase. Just before reaching the door, Lexia Dryden arrived before them.

"Well done, Abdul," she commended him, staring at Sebastian. "I've wanted to meet you—for a very long time. Both of you—follow me."

He felt Abdul's grip on him suddenly tighten as he was shoved through the doorway into a dimly lit stairwell. Straining to be let go proved useless as he was no match for Abdul's strength, who continued tightening his hold of him. Scotty's dad remained expressionless as they reached the floor below. Entering a dark hallway, they followed Lexia to an elevator and waited until the doors opened. "*I— trusted—you,*" Sebastian gasped out, watching Abdul's face which failed to offer any reaction. Lexia smirked, staying silent.

Once inside, Sebastian felt nauseous as the elevator plummeted. Noticing the tremor of his left hand, his heart nearly stopped when Abdul gently began massaging it. With his chest heaving for breath, he looked up at Abdul, who now stared back at him. And while his face remained expressionless, his eyes seemed softer, offering Sebastian a glimmer of hope. Was he actually trying to help?

***

"*Your daughter—was a robot*?" Scotty uttered, disbelief dripping from each word.

"A synthetic replicate," Lee responded, resting his hand on Scotty's shoulder as the two looked down at Lydia and Gideon.

Then searching out through the scurrying crowd, Scotty grew panicked. "Sebastian's gone! He was just standing by the window!"

"Lexia's gone, too," Lee added. "Come on! Follow me!"

Rushing down the staircase, together they pressed through the crowd until Scotty collided with Xavier. "Dad! Have you seen Sebastian?"

"No. I don't even know where Abdul is," he fretted.

"We need to find Sebastian." Scotty desperately turned to Lee who stood still, glancing off toward the staircase.

"I think I know where they are—or at least where they're going," he blankly said. "Come on!" Following close behind, Scotty kept pace with Lee until they reached a gray door near the staircase and then headed into the emergency stairwell. With the sounds of their shoes echoing off the metal stairs, they quickly found the first door on the lower level. After running down a dimly lit hallway, they came to an elevator, a red light showing it in use. "They're heading for the executive conference room. We can take the executive elevator down here at the end of the hallway. This way."

Sprinting to the hallway's end, Lee quickly entered numbers onto a keypad to access the elevator. Once inside, Lee spoke out, "Subterranean level four."

A male monotone voice responded through the overhead speaker, "Please step up to the control panel for eye scan confirmation." Following the instructions, Lee allowed both eyes to be scanned. The elevator then began its descent.

"We need to go to the executive conference room!" Scotty protested.

Resting his hand on Scotty's shoulder, Lee responded, "We will—but there's something I need to get first." Moving away, Scotty watched as Lee pounded in anger against an interior wall, then resting his back against it exhaling his frustration. Closing his eyes, he appeared lost in his thoughts.

Hesitantly, Scotty asked, "Did you know about Lydia being a—*synthetic*—*replicate*?"

Without looking at him, Lee blankly answered, "When Lydia turned ten years old, she became obsessed with robotics, learning everything she could. By fifteen, she had designed her first robot...and by eighteen—she began working in our artificial intelligence division—on replicates so much more advanced than anyone could imagine."

"And—she built one—in her own image," Scotty commented, confirmed by Lee's nod. "Why?"

"She's attempting to gain control of the company— by any means possible."

"So—where is the real Lydia?"

"I'm not sure," Lee responded, opening his eyes, staring off. "Several months ago she and I fought after—"

"After what?"

"After—this."

Upon the opening of the elevator door, a boy, roughly Scotty's age, dressed in blue jeans and a black T-shirt, stood there waiting for them.

"Dad, I missed you," he said, smiling.

"Hello, Joshua," Lee greeted him, looking wearily at Scotty.

"Is this your *son*?" Scotty asked with confusion. "Wait! He's not—"

"A synthetic replicate," Lee responded, walking past Lydia's creation, having the uncanny appearance of a much younger version of Lee Dryden.

***

Shuddering as Abdul forced him to sit in a chair, Sebastian glanced forward out through the windows showing the glittering night skyline of San Francisco. As breathtaking as usual, he instantly picked up that something was off as he watched two helicopters speed through the view. The tightness of Abdul's firm grip on his shoulders fed his anxiety and racing pulse, the faint reflection on Lexia Dryden moving closer made his heart nearly burst through his chest.

"You, young man, are a means to an end," she casually stated, walking in front of him and then leaning back against a large black desk. "I expect your father will be here in a moment—for a long overdue reunion."

Without knocking, the office door opened with Lee Dryden slowly stepping inside. Sebastian noticed his reflection upon the dark windows as he remained near the door. "*Well*, aren't you going to say hello to your son?" Lexia asked, entwining her fingers and resting her hands against her thighs.

His reply both confused and frightened Sebastian. "That's not my son."

Abruptly standing up straight and appearing to lose her patience, Lexia replied, "Liar."

"Joshua, will you come in here?" Lee requested. Sebastian's eyes grew larger upon seeing the reflection of a boy his age enter and approach Lee Dryden. "I'll have to thank the *real* Lydia someday for helping me find him."

Lexia seemed startled by this but held her composure. Nodding her head, she whispered, "Abdul."

Swiftly restraining Sebastian with a choke hold, with his other hand Abdul pressed the barrel of a gun against his head. Quaking with terror, Sebastian burst out crying, unable to speak any words as he gasped for air. Through his light-headedness, though, he felt Abdul's hold gently lessen and noticed how his fingertips began tapping against him, maybe offering him a sign.

"Let that boy go. He has nothing to do with you and me," Lee urged.

"Well, I simply can't do that now—due to this Arab fool failing to bring me the right boy. This young man has seen too much. Such a pity," she coldly finished.

"Dad, what's going on?" Joshua asked.

Smirking, Lexia answered, "Your father has committed something highly regrettable."

"What's done—is done. There's no going back now," Lee offered. "They're coming for you. You and the rest of them."

Turning away, Lexia uttered, "You've ruined everything. Do you have any idea what you have done? The turmoil you unleashed tonight will have staggering effects across the globe. You have opened all of us up to unimaginable retributions."

Calmly, he responded, "I know *exactly* what I've done. It's what I should have done a long time ago. I'm just as guilty as you are—by letting things happen." Stepping forward, he added, "There's no escape. I warned you—but you and the others refused to stop. You went too far. And now—they'll find you—and when they do—God help your soul."

"That was your true failing, my dearest husband," she said, stepping up to Sebastian and Abdul. "You always believed—I had a soul." Reaching out, Lexia ripped the gun from Abdul's grasp and fired at Joshua. His head instantly exploded with an array of sparks, sending him sprawling to the floor, violently convulsing until the last of his power was spent with smoke rising from his head. Lexia's hands covered her mouth in apparent shock.

Releasing Sebastian, Abdul lunged for Lexia, forcing her down, banging her head against the floor as he wrestled the gun from her. Choking her with his bare hands, Lee dragged him away after she'd fallen unconscious. "They need to find her alive," Lee warned. "She—needs to—pay for—what—she's—done," he panted, falling to his knees as Abdul rolled off her.

Staggering up off the chair, Sebastian looked worryingly at both of them. Trembling in fear, he stepped back toward the windows, keeping his eyes on them. Thinking fast about running for the open door, he held still when Scotty appeared in the doorway. His friend's hands were outstretched as he started approaching him. "It's okay," Scotty kept repeating.

Glancing away, seeing Abdul grinning at him, Sebastian backed up further until he felt the window behind him. With the sounds of sirens from outside resounding in his ears, he stumbled forward when another helicopter sped by the windows. Sebastian watched as Lee Dryden approached him. With their eyes locked on each other, he saw tears falling from Lee's eyes as Lee reached over, tenderly touching his cheek. Swallowing hard, Sebastian forced out, "Are you—my dad?"

"Yeah," Lee answered, nervously smiling while pulling Sebastian to him. "I'm so sorry," Lee whispered in his ear, kissing him on his cheek, his beard lightly touching his skin, something he remembered from a long time ago. Growing light-headed, Sebastian heard Lee call his name as everything went dark.

Chapter Ten

Opening his eyes, he glanced up at his dad's lightly bearded face. With his cheek resting against his dad's white shirt, Sebastian felt the thumping of his heart next to his ear. Feeling someone tuck a blanket closer around him, he looked over, seeing Xavier smile at him. "Where are we?" he softly asked.

Looking down, his dad quietly answered, "We're driving across the Golden Gate Bridge, heading north out of the city." Feeling his dad hold him closer, Sebastian tried to close his eyes, but they kept opening.

"Where's Scotty?"

"I'm up here," he heard his friend say from one of the front seats.

"What about Abdul?"

"I'm driving, my friend," Abdul answered. "Trust me, we're all safe. Go back to sleep. It will be a while before get to where we're going."

"I'm sorry you were so scared," his dad apologized. "Abdul has been working for me in secret for years. He would never have hurt you." Sebastian noticed Abdul wink at him through the rearview mirror.

Restfully exhaling, Sebastian noticed the tremor coursing through his hand until his dad grabbed hold, stilling the trembling as best he could.

"Lee," he heard Abdul call out.

Sensing the car was slowing down, Sebastian sat up, looking out the dark windows at the lights of traffic passing by.

"Someone has hacked into the car's navigational system," Abdul tried to calmly say, but Sebastian recognized frustration, and maybe even concern in his tone.

"I got this," Scotty mumbled while typing commands into the navigation console. Within a minute the car returned to Abdul's control. "Someone definitely accessed the corporate navigation software, wanting to turn us around. And I think that someone—is calling right now."

A blinking light on the dashboard confirmed an incoming message, the name appearing on the screen, *Lydia Dryden*. Sighing, Lee uttered, "Receive call." His daughter's picture appeared on-screen, with her looking exactly the same as when Sebastian first met her at One Legacy Place.

"Hello, Daddy."

"Lydia."

"All the social media sights have shown mother being arrested." Lee kept looking at the screen without saying anything about this. "How could you unleash Nightfall? You ruined everything."

"I did what I had to do," he calmly answered.

"Reports are coming in from all over the world, riots in Paris and Berlin, protests in Tokyo and Sydney, our embassy stormed in Athens. The Russians and Chinese are calling on the President to resign. What will happen in the morning when people find out all the secrets everyone has kept? Some—have already gone into hiding."

"They'll be found."

"What about me? I'm your daughter."

Growling through his teeth, Lee rasped, "You stopped being my daughter when—" He stopped himself from finishing his sentence, glancing at Sebastian.

"Tell him, Daddy. I can see him there with you. Tell him what I tried to do."

Looking to his dad, feeling scared, Sebastian waited for his response.

"End call," Lee responded. The screen went black.

Staring ahead, finding a reassuring smile from Scotty, Sebastian quietly asked, "What is Nightfall?"

Looking to him with a sad sort of grin, his dad replied, "The truth."

***

Arriving just before sunrise, Abdul pulled the car off the road. Everyone stiffly climbed out, stretching their legs and massaging their backs and necks. "Over here," Lee pointed. Walking in the direction of the ocean, they found flights of steps leading down cliffs to the beach below. Warm gusts of salty air blew against them as they treaded across the cool sand. Watching crabs scurrying away from the rolling waves, Sebastian also saw seagulls soaring overhead in the pinkish-orange sky.

Just up the beach from them, he noticed a small bungalow with a wrap-around porch, some beach chairs and a hammock. Wrapped in strong arms from behind him, Sebastian felt his dad's beard with his head resting on his shoulder. "We're almost home," he heard his dad say over the sounds of the waves.

"This isn't it?" Sebastian asked with surprise.

"No. We need to go a little farther."

***

"So, what exactly is this place?" Scotty asked as they stepped inside. High ceilings, painted white, contrasted against teal-colored walls and wicker furniture in the living and dining spaces. A spacious kitchen, three large bedrooms, and one decent–sized bathroom, in truth, made the bungalow seem larger inside that it did from the outside.

With them all gathering around the kitchen island, Lee revealed, "I bought this place after I graduated from Stanford. It's been my secret hideout for years." Looking at Sebastian, he continued, "Your mom was the only other person who knew about this place. It's where you started, " he added with a grin.

"This place has never shown up in the corporate real estate listings," Xavier confirmed.

"And it never will. I paid cash for it." From his pocket, Lee pulled out the key, handing it to Xavier. "Now it's yours."

"*What*?" he responded, completely surprised.

"Follow me," Lee said, leading them all down a hallway to the last door. Stepping inside the room, he motioned for them to gather around a large armoire. Pulling on the doors, he opened it up, revealing a Daybreak chamber inside."

"I thought the other one was at your home in Silicon Valley," Abdul noted.

"After Lydia disposed of its twin at One Legacy Place, I secretly had mine moved here."

"Won't there be records of the move?" Scotty asked.

Smiling, Lee answered, "Not when you pay movers from Chinatown triple the rate under the table." Returning the conversation to the bungalow being a gift, Lee continued, addressing Abdul, Xavier, and Scotty. "Things in San Francisco and other cities are going to get bad, *really* bad. It's not safe to be there. But this place is. Everything you need is here, money in the safe, untraceable internet via satellite and some pretty awesome computer equipment in the next room. I want the three of you to stay here—as caretakers for the house—and for Sebastian and me." Shifting his attention to his son, Lee sighed, saying, "You and I need to escape for a while—because—"

"I have Parkinson's disease," Sebastian interrupted.

"You know?" Lee uttered, seeing Scotty's surprise as well. "How?"

"I found out before I ran away from the boys home. I didn't want it to be true. I kept denying it to myself—but I can't anymore."

Tenderly touching his son's cheek, Lee softly said, "I'll take care of you. I promise."

***

The night breeze wisped against the roaring flames of their beach fire, as they enjoyed their final night together. Looking to his dad, Sebastian asked, "I still don't understand about Nightfall."

Poking the fire with a stick, Lee explained, "Throughout the years, the government had not only been spying on the citizens here in our country but in other countries as well. Spying itself is nothing new—but that changed a few years ago—when Dryden's Artificial Intelligence Division obtained a secret contract with the government in the development of a new breed of spies, synthetic replicates, or highly advanced robots. I begged the board of directors to pass on the contract, but Lexia spearheaded their acceptance. After the first models were developed, the government successfully tested the program by replacing the President of Liberia with a synthetic double after his last trip to the UN in New York. From that point on, the conspiracy of replacing world leaders with these sophisticated spies went global."

"*Unbelievable*," Scotty mumbled.

Continuing, Lee revealed, "Then the government unleashed the synthetic replicates here in our country, replacing political rivals and activists, outspoken public figures, and such. When I authorized the release of Nightfall, the hidden records of this program were sent to every mobile device in our country and to news agencies around the world."

"How is it—that a program—so damaging in the scope of the criminal information it involves—was so easily accessed—and disbursed like a balloon with the air being let out of it? Xavier asked.

"Because they used software designed by Dryden," Lee confirmed, now looking to Scotty. "They believed that all incriminating evidence was deleted after each replicate assumed the identity of the person being replaced. The software is, however, designed to hold the information for a designated period of time before deletion. I was able to access the information, copying it to encrypted files with the use of—"

"Crumbs," Scotty supplied the last word. "You found them by the crumbs they left."

Noticing Xavier's confusion, Abdul leaned over to him, whispering, "I'll explain it later."

"Why didn't you try to stop it sooner?" Scotty then asked.

"I can answer that," Abdul interrupted, glancing knowingly at Lee. "A codicil to the government contract states that anyone who authorizes the information's release will be charged with treason and espionage--and would be shot by firing squad, without a trial. You, my friend, have forfeited your life in the name of the truth." Nodding his head, Lee silently confirmed this.

***

Resting his back against the interior wall of the Daybreak, Sebastian placed the headphones over his ears, hearing a slight humming sound. His dad attached heart monitors over both his nipples and an even longer, additional monitor over his heart, capable of offering electric shocks should it stop beating. A breathing tube was also positioned under his nostrils and his wrist was wrapped for gauging his pulse. His dad then softly touched his cheek, smiling, "All this stuff is going to monitor your vital signs. If something goes wrong, the program will stop—and you'll wake up.

"How long will we be asleep?"

"As long as it lets us. Hopefully—for a long time." Leaning in, his dad kissed him on the forehead. "I love you, kiddo." Nervously grinning, Sebastian exhaled.

After Abdul attached similar health monitors to his dad, Lee grabbed hold of his hand, hearing him say, "I'll see you in Maine."

Sebastian smiled bigger until he glanced out the glass door at Scotty. Swallowing deep, the thought of leaving his only friend, even for just a short time, broke his heart, which was clearly reflected back from Scotty. "I'll see you sometime," he called out, forcing a tense sigh from Scotty. Reaching out, he pressed his fist against the glass, seeing his friend reluctantly smile and do the same. Although he couldn't hear him through the glass door, Sebastian understood the word Scotty said to him, nodding his head, letting him know this.

After one final glance between them, Scotty slowly closed the armoire doors, plunging the Daybreak into darkness. Breathing in deep, he felt his dad tighten their grip on his hand. Closing his eyes, Sebastian inhaled deeply, releasing his breath as his ears captured the sound of waves crashing in on the shore.

The brisk sensation of water flowing over his feet awakened Sebastian from what seemed like a trance. Squinting for a moment, his eyes adjusted to the light, as he saw a pelican skimming over the water before diving in to capture a fish. Stretching a bit, Sebastian stood up, realizing his clothes had changed back to blue jeans rolled up to his knees and a blue-checkered unbuttoned plaid shirt. Before he could take a step, strong arms embraced him from behind. "Welcome home, kiddo," he heard his dad say, feeling a soft beard against his cheek. Then hearing his dad say, "Let's go check this place out," Sebastian turned, greeted by his dad's beaming smile, as the wind blew strands of his dad's longish hair over his eyes.

"I love you," he said to Sebastian.

"I love you, too, Dad."

**

Sometime during the night, Sebastian rolled over in bed, hearing the tranquil droning of waves washing up on shore. Easing out of bed, he left his bedroom, walking down the hallway to his dad's door. Looking in, he saw his dad sleeping on his stomach with moonlight flooding through the window over his bed. Hearing his dad's light restful snore made him feel safe. Stepping through the doorway, he sought a better look at the tattoo on the back of his dad's shoulder, a colorful kite.

Not wanting to wake him, Sebastian quietly backed out of the room and headed for the door at the end of the hallway. Entering into the lighthouse tower, he cautiously climbed the dark circular staircase, lit only with moonlight from two small windows. He heard only the sounds of his bare feet slapping the floor as he headed to the top. Once he stepped out, gusting wind brushed forcefully against his ears.

Glancing up, the moon looked so close he thought he might be able to reach out and touch it. He thought the same about the stars, having never seen so many before. The moon's rays fell on the offshore fog bank, causing it to look like luminescent veils, almost ghost-like. Yet from his vantage point, Sebastian spied something in the distance that he couldn't take his eyes off, a faint light he recognized, thinking of it with only one word, *back door*. Sitting down, Sebastian dangled his feet over the edge as he rested his chest against the black railing. He continued watching the light for hours—until the sky surrendered its hold of the night to the brilliance of a red-colored dawn.

Part Two
Dusk

Chapter Eleven

"I think a storm is coming," Sebastian's dad commented as they walked along the beach after a refreshing swim in the cool ocean. Pointing toward the lighthouse, he continued, "Look how the waves are crashing into the rocks. I've never seen the sea so disturbed here." Sebastian glanced out toward the surf, watching the whitecaps. Since escaping here with his dad, the sky was always clear, having never rained once.

"Were storms part of your program when you designed it?"

Looking out at the sea and the ever-present fog bank shrouding the distance, Lee replied, "No. The program I developed scanned both your mom's and my memories of our time when we first came here to the lighthouse. The weather was beautiful the entire week, blue skies with a few white fair weather clouds passing over occasionally during the day and night skies filled with stars."

"So why is the storm coming?" Sebastian asked, feeling growing unease inside him.

His dad must have sensed this, wrapping him in his strong wet arms. "It'll be okay, kiddo. *Possibly*—your mom or me had thought about a storm sometime during that week—and the program scanned this into the database? Or possibly it's something as simple as a software anomaly, what some people like to call '*a ghost in the machine*'."

Feeling his dad's soft beard against his cheek always made Sebastian feel safe. The tranquility and carefreeness this place exuded was exactly what he needed after experiencing the harshness and brutality that San

Francisco had succumbed to. Yet he could not help worrying about Scotty and his dads, hoping they were safe and missing them.

Finding a place to sit on the beach, he took a moment to just stare out at the water before he glanced over at his dad. He wanted to know something but was feeling nervous about approaching the topic. "What was mom like? You mention her now-and-then but—I don't remember anything about her—and I feel bad about that."

"Don't. It's not your fault that you can't remember her." Scooting closer to him, his dad leaned against him. Sighing, he slicked his long brown hair back. Lee then answered, "She loved you—more than you could imagine. Her smile would just beam every time she held you. Aside from being beautiful, Melinda was the smartest woman I ever met because she could see through all the unnecessary stuff and focus on the important things. She didn't care about money or possessions. I think that all she wanted— was to love you and me." Pulling him closer, his dad finished, "And she did."

The darkening colors out in the ocean returned his thoughts to the coming storm, as he anxiously wondered if something was going wrong. Glimpsing down at his hand, Sebastian watched it calmly resting at his side unable to remember the last time a tremor gripped it. He hadn't experienced any symptoms of Parkinson's disease since arriving. Desperately wanting everything to be okay, he closed his eyes, trying only to think of much happier thoughts of him and his dad here together. However, the faint sound of thunder echoing from far out at sea seemed to affirm that it would not so easily be dismissed.

Hypnotized by the rolling waves and the seagulls flying over the ocean swells, they both just sat there, staring out at the white sea foam washing up over their feet. Standing up, Sebastian noticed how the overhead clouds had grown darker and appeared to be moving faster. Luring him away from watching, he heard his dad say, "I'm starving. Let's go make some dinner and then later we can sit by the fire and I'll tell you more about your mom."

"Sounds good," he said, smiling, hoping he'd convinced his dad he wasn't worried anymore about the coming storm, which was far from the truth.

***

A loud clap of thunder jarred Sebastian from his sleep. Rolling over stretching, his eyes were drawn to the three flashes of lightning playing across the ceiling. Reaching over for the alarm clock on his nightstand, he checked the time. He'd been asleep for three hours. Feeling more tired than when he crawled in bed, Sebastian rolled onto his stomach, dragging his pillow over his head.

An explosion of thunder, strong enough to shake his bed, forced Sebastian fully awake. Rising from his bed, he spied out his window through the curtains. Bursts of lightning caused him to squint, unable to fully see what it was like outside. Wanting to go back to bed, he hesitated, deciding instead to crawl into bed with his dad.

Stepping out into the hallway, he heard the droning ticks of a clock perched on the mantle in the living room, between the roar of the thunder. Treading lightly down to his dad's open bedroom door, Sebastian peered in, finding him missing from his bed. Turning back, he passed by the open bathroom door before heading to the kitchen. Again, there were no signs of him.

Sebastian sat down at the table to think for a moment of where he might have gone. He didn't believe he would go outside during the storm, but his dad could have gone to the lighthouse. Maybe he'd gone up there to check on the storm's approach. A minute later, standing at the foot of the iron spiral staircase leading to the top of the lighthouse, an uneasy feeling, turning his stomach, gripped him. Taking a deep breath, he started climbing the steps, clenching the railing to steady himself as the continuing thunder shook it.

Once at the top, Sebastian shielded his eyes from the blinding light's rotation as he stepped out onto the observation deck. Forced back against the clear glass windows by heavy gusts of wind, he found it hard to breathe with the pressure against his chest and the wind-driven rain pelting his skin. The deafening roar of the ocean swell left his ears aching. Partially covering his eyes with his hand, he looked out, seeing several bolts of lightning striking the ocean surface, feeling their charge in the air. As frightening as the raging storm appeared, something else caught his eyes and left him feeling anxious and almost light-headed. Off in the far distance where he'd seen the constant light, this beacon he believed as being the program's back door, the light was now rapidly blinking.

***

Opening his eyes, Lee heard the soft buzzing hum from his headphones. Disoriented at first, he grew panicked, reaching out through the darkness, feeling the Daybreak's glass door in front of him. With his heart rapidly beating and his pulse racing, he yanked the heart monitors off his chest and freed himself from the breathing tube and pulse monitor on his hand. Finding the inner door handle, he pushed the door open, forcing open the armoire doors as well.

Searching for the room's light switch, once the overhead light flickered on, he turned back to the Daybreak chamber. Sebastian appeared still asleep, his breathing even and undisturbed. Sighing with relief, Lee gently touched his son's check and lightly ran his fingers through his hair.

As he was stepping over to a desk to access information on two laptop computers, the bedroom door opened with Abdul and Scotty rushing inside. "Lee, what are you doing awake?" Abdul asked. Scotty had moved passed them, typing access codes into both computers.

"I don't know why I'm awake," he answered, moving behind Scotty and looking over his shoulder.

"And Sebastian?"

"He's still asleep. What do his vital signs show?" Lee asked Scotty.

"Everything normal, pulse, heart rate, respiration. He's fine."

"What about my vital signs before I woke up?"

"Normal, *everything*."

"Then why am I awake?"

Entering more commands in the second laptop, Scotty responded, "We'll know in a minute. I'm running a diagnostic on the Daybreak." With the results slowly scrolling on the screen, Scotty pointed to something troubling. "There, see? The firewall was breached. Someone gained remote access to the software, logging into only *your* data—which terminated the program for you."

"Can you trace the source of the breach?" Abdul asked.

After typing for almost a minute, Scotty turned to them both. "No. The connection is untraceable. I'll tell you this; whoever hacked into this system knew what they were doing."

"How so?" Abdul questioned, resting his hand on Scotty's shoulder.

"To gain access to the system, the hacker needed to channel their spying through the remote satellite, not an easy task. Then they needed to break through the firewall to gain access to the database. And from there—they had to decipher the software, targeting only you, Lee."

"Is it possible that—"

"Lydia?" Lee interrupted Abdul. "Knowing how intelligent she is with designing synthetic replicates—I'd say she's probably the one who hacked us—or showed someone else how to do it. What about the program now?"

Typing more commands, Scotty answered, "I'll repair the firewall and add more protection to the system. That's the best I can do."

Xavier appeared in the doorway, looking surprised and concerned all at once, Lee asked, "How long was I asleep?"

"A week yesterday," Abdul confirmed.

"And—what's been happening since we went to sleep?"

Sighing, Abdul revealed, "Anti-American demonstrations have broken out across the world, the most severe being in Europe. Here, at home, anti-government riots are a daily occurrence in most major cities. Martial law has been implemented in Miami, Chicago, Los Angeles, and San Francisco, among others. The authorities have abandoned New York, such is the chaos there. The Canadians are allowing refugees to cross the border, provided they can prove they aren't replicates. Mexico has closed its border."

"And—what is the government doing about the replicates?"

"Bowing to public pressure, the replicates are being destroyed as soon as they're found—and anyone harboring a replicate faces arrest—if not worse," Abdul answered.

"I should make us some coffee," Xavier uttered, quickly disappearing.

Exchanging concerned glances, Abdul mumbled, "I'll go help him."

Nervously pacing across the room, Lee once more checked on Sebastian before stepping out into the hallway. Hearing the sounds of the tide rolling up on shore, he moved further toward the kitchen, stopping when he saw Abdul ease up behind Xavier near the coffee pot. "You need water for that," Abdul said, noticing that Xavier failed to fill the carafe.

"I'm sorry," Xavier uttered only a moment before blinding light flooded into the house from every window with the deafening sounds of helicopters echoing closer.

Chapter Twelve

Staggering back inside, Sebastian fought to catch his breath, his body quaking with fear. Yet when doing so, he breathed in the unmistakable stench of something burning with no visible traces of smoke. Descending a few steps down into the darkness of the lighthouse tower, he collapsed against the wall, overcome by light-headedness with everything spinning in sight. His pulse and heartbeat accelerated when what he saw began to pixelate and distort, just as it did the last time before he returned to the real world after being inside the Daybreak. Gripped with terror, all he could do was watch as the circular staircase below him faded away with everything around him turning pitch black.

The resounding thunderation of the storm grew silent, yet the pungent odor of smoke intensified. Gathering his thoughts, Sebastian reached out, instantly pulling his hands back after singeing his fingers on something he couldn't see. He could also feel the heat radiating from the floor under his bare feet. Reaching his hands up, he felt the headphones covering his ears. Pulling them and his breathing tube off, his hand traced down to his chest, peeling the heart monitors off his skin.

Opening his eyes, Sebastian spotted a crack in the darkness before him, allowing a sliver of light to penetrate into the Daybreak. Again reaching out, he cautiously touched the door handle with his fingertips. It seemed to have bent almost as if melted.

"Dad, are you awake?" he anxiously asked, only then realizing he was alone. Frightened by this, he grasped the hot door handle, forcing the door open. The blackness before him quickly disintegrated to ash, revealing the charred, smoky remains of the house that once stood around the Daybreak. In the palm of his outstretched hand, Sebastian captured blown ash, reminding him of snow. The strong breezes gusting inland off the ocean picked up the ash, creating a blackish-gray flurry.

"Dad! Scotty! Abdul! Xavier!" Frantically yelling out for each of them over the sounds of waves rolling onto the beach, no one responded to his calls. "Where are you?" he breathlessly whispered, feeling more scared than ever before. Coughing from the smoke he breathed in, Sebastian teetered dizzily for a second—resting his hand against the Daybreak. He quickly pulled it back after burning his palm against the surface.

Careful where he walked, Sebastian's jaw dropped, both heartsick and awed by how little was left of the house. All the computers had melted as well as the desk they sat on. The kitchen appliances appeared as black boxes amidst the heaping piles of what remained of the wooden structure. The claw-foot bathtub had been darkly glazed over, the only surviving remnant of the bathroom. Looking down, he saw how the scorched floors were cracking and falling apart under his weight.

On unsteady legs, Sebastian found his way out to the beach, glancing back at what remained of the bungalow. Loud creaking sounds were followed by the floor collapsing, toppling over the Daybreak, which exploded with a shower of sparks. Swallowing deep, Sebastian fell to his knees, overwhelmed that the link to the lighthouse was gone forever and that he was alone, having no clue of what happened to his dad and friends.

***

"I'm—sorry," Xavier murmured through his tears. Facing away from him, Abdul extended his arms, comfortingly rubbing the backs of both Scotty and Lee. "Say something, *please*!" He begged to the three of them.

Through his hands covering his face, Lee quietly responded, "What did Lydia promise you—in return for betraying us?"

Sobbing uncontrollably, Xavier answered, "She—p-promised—that—Abdul and Scotty and I—w-would be—s-safe."

"Do you feel safe?" Abdul evenly asked, clearly holding in his anger, staring forward.

"Abdul, I—" Xavier's words trailed off, seeming unable to offer an answer.

Bursting out with his own tears, Scotty covered his eyes with his hand. He felt someone take hold of his other hand, looking down he saw that it was Lee's hand covering his. "Sebastian should be okay—as long as he didn't come out of the Daybreak when the house was burning. None of the government agents went inside before they torched the place."

"After we went outside with our hands in the air, wouldn't they have noticed he wasn't with us?" Scotty uttered.

"A *mistake* on their part?" Abdul wondered.

Looking away, Lee deeply exhaled out, "I don't think so. Lydia would have wanted Sebastian to suffer more than any of us. What could be worse than being burned alive?"

"You said the Daybreak was fireproof. Wouldn't she have known this?" Scotty asked, wiping his tears away.

Weakly grinning, Lee confessed, "The Daybreak's original designs never provided this information –should anyone have been looking for it." Gripping Scotty's hand tighter, Lee added, "He's okay. I just know he is."

"How very—*touching*," Lexia's comment sounded out from the darkest corner of the cell across from theirs. Stepping into the dim light, Lee's jaw dropped, witnessing the disheveled appearance of his wife, wearing the same dress she'd worn the night of the party at One Legacy Place and with smeared makeup on her face. The one thing she'd maintained, however, was her frigidness. "Well, well, I never imagined seeing my husband in a cell across from mine—although in recent days I may have hoped it would happen."

"A pleasure to see you, as well," Lee dryly greeted her without getting up from his seat.

"You have, however, spoiled *everything* for me, now that I know who they will kill first," she further taunted.

"As long as I never have to hear or see you again, I'm good with that," Lee responded.

"I believe the lethal injection is being prepared as we speak," Lexia continued. "*Although*—should they decide to use a firing squad or electrocution, I would not object to any last minute changes in their procedure."

"Yes, you would," Lee disputed her words. "Your only regret—is that you're not the one injecting me or pulling the trigger—and that Lydia won't be standing there waiting for her turn."

"Sometimes I forget how well you know me," Lexia admitted, slowly backing away, returning to the darkest corner of her cell, speaking no more to her husband.

The loud noise made by the main cellblock door opening at the far end of the hallway preceded the almost deliberately slow sounds of people walking toward them. Looking up, Lee watched as Lydia stepped into the light in front of their cell, accompanied by one of the prison guards. "All of you to the back of the cell *now*!" the guard demanded. All reluctantly complied.

Turning toward Xavier, Lydia smiled at him, "You're free to go."

"What?" he gasped.

"I promised you that if you helped with the arrest of my father—I would let you go," she responded with an airy lilt in her voice.

"What about Abdul and Scotty?" Xavier frantically asked.

"I'm staying," Abdul answered, maintaining his anger staring away from Xavier.

"Me, too," Scotty added. Lydia continued to smile, saying nothing regarding their decision to stay. Once more bursting out in tears, Xavier was grabbed by the guard who dragged him from the cell, locking the door behind him. Sobbing profusely, he was led away with Lydia following behind, having said nothing to her parents.

"I'm sorry, Dad," Scotty whispered, resting his head against Abdul's shoulder.

"As am I," Abdul calmly responded.

***

Sitting on the beach next to a fire he'd made, Sebastian watched the moon's fluid reflection on the ocean's surface. Glancing up, he gazed upon stars too numerous to count in the clear night sky. As impressive as all this should have seemed, none of it mattered to him. He'd spent the day searching through the charred ruins of the bungalow as well as the surrounding beach, trying to find anything revealing what happened to his dad and Scotty and his dads. If they had left a trail in the sand, then the strong sea breeze gusting onshore saw to hiding this from him.

Guessing they might have been taken by someone back to San Francisco, and not knowing how far away that was, left him feeling helpless. He'd thought about returning to the city in the electric car that had brought them here, but the car was missing. He'd also thought about hitchhiking, which was against the law. But he never really believed that most drivers wouldn't stop for a teenager only wearing a pair of black pants. Wanting to just curl up and cry, he knew he was too exhausted to even do that.

A distant light and the unfamiliar sound of what he thought might be an engine suddenly drew his attention down the dark beach. With both the light and sound coming closer, Sebastian stood up, holding a stick in his hand, ready to fight if he needed to. Speeding toward him, the light went out, as the intruder approached, keeping him hidden until the glow of Sebastian's fire revealed all.

Slowing to a stop across the fire from him was what appeared to be a dirt bike emerging from the darkness. Wearing a black jacket and pants with his face hidden behind a helmet, the rider got off the bike, reaching up to pull the helmet off.

To Sebastian's surprise, the rider was a pretty Chinese girl, having long, flowing hair. "I can't believe I actually found you," she said, smiling.

Lowering his stick, Sebastian cautiously asked, "Who are you?"

"I'm Nikki. Scotty sent me."

"Scotty! Is he okay? What about my dad? Where are they? What happened to them?" Sebastian rapidly asked question after question, not giving her a chance to answer any.

"Hold on," she said, taking a step toward him. He backed away.

"It's okay. I'm not going to hurt you. You don't have to be afraid."

"I'm not—afraid," Sebastian unconvincingly responded.

"Your hand says different," Nikki commented. Looking down, Sebastian noticed the tremor coursing through his hand, only now realizing his Parkinson's had returned.

"I'll tell you what I know. Scotty and I have been online friends for a couple of years now. During the night, he sent me an urgent message, giving me this location and the name *Sebastian*, which is your name, right?"

"Yeah."

"The only other words he texted were *help* and *home*. I'm sorry it took so long to get here. I live up in Oregon. It took me hours to find you."

"Where—is here?"

"According to my GPS, we're on the northern California coast just a few miles from McKinleyville." Slowly stepping closer, Nikki offered, "I'm here to help—but I'm not sure how."

Thinking for a moment about what she said, "I know where he wants us to go—if you're sure about this?"

"I am. I made a promise to him. I never go back on my promises." Stepping closer, she pulled off her jacket, handing it to him. "It's too cold to ride shirtless—and I intend to go *fast*."

"Thanks," Sebastian said, his shyness showing through as he took it from her.

Returning to her dirt bike, she climbed on, saying, "Let's get going." Walking over to her, he hesitated getting on, not sure what he needed to do. Before he could react, she pulled his hands to her waist. "Are you gonna shake like that the whole time?" she asked, referring to his hand. Smiling at him, she added, "I'm not that pretty."

"Yes, you are," he blurted out, then with embarrassment in his tone corrected himself, "I mean, I—can't help it."

"Okay," she said, grinning. "So where are we going?"

"San Francisco."

Appearing stunned, she asked, "Are you sure? There are some really bad things going on there"

"Yeah, we need to—*please*."

Chapter Thirteen

Feeling nauseated by her bold weaving through heavy traffic, Sebastian's heart sank when San Francisco finally came into view. Although he'd seen it shrouded in fog several times, he'd never seen the skyline veiled with billowing smoke from numerous fires. Yet piercing through the gray cloud hovering over the city, One Legacy Place shone its towering presence as if defiantly demanding to be seen.

Pulling the dirt bike off onto the roadside as traffic came to a halt, Nikki turned off the engine as Sebastian took off the helmet. "Why are we stopping?"

"Security checkpoints are set up at the other end of the bridge. Everyone entering the city is being searched before they're allowed to continue on. I don't think they'll let two runaways into the city," Nikki responded.

"I didn't know you were a runaway?"

"That's how Scotty and I met," Nikki revealed. "We were both sent to this camp for troubled teens in Utah—about three years ago. After we finished the program, I went back to my foster parents in Oregon and Scotty eventually got adopted by a gay couple in San Francisco."

"I met them. They're nice," Sebastian commented.

"Anyway, if you want to get into the city, we're going to have to hitch a ride."

"That's illegal."

Grinning, Nikki answered, "Yeah, it is."

Pulling up near them, a black security cruiser stopped. An officer stepped out to look ahead at how far back the traffic was. Spying from behind a minivan, Nikki led Sebastian through the traffic until he stopped dead in his tracks. His eyes fixed solidly on the security officer who hadn't noticed him. Sebastian just stood there, unable to take his eyes off him. He was the same one who had stared at him the night of the riot they witnessed on their way to One Legacy Place. Remembering everything about his face, Sebastian wanted to run away but Nikki continued pulling on his hand.

Shaking his head, almost bursting into tears, Sebastian grew even more frightened when Nikki motioned toward the security cruiser, understanding her intentions. Gripping his hand, she reassuringly nodded her head, silently encouraging him to follow her. Believing this was suicide, he reluctantly followed her.

Over the sounds of horns being blown by frustrated drivers, Nikki and Sebastian snuck over to the cruiser, climbing into the backseat and crouching down on the floor. Fighting to keep his breathing shallow, fearing being found, Sebastian nearly panicked when the office got back inside and began driving again, oblivious to his stowaways. Nikki's continuous rubbing of the back of his trembling hand only slightly eased his distress.

As the cruiser drove faster, the only thing Sebastian could think of was never seeing his dad again. Everything was so confusing and overwhelming. Closing his eyes, he fought off thoughts in his mind about what had and could happen, concentrating instead on the chatter sounding out from the dashboard speaker. Call after call for assistance flooded the channel, ranging from common domestic disputes to unlawful entry to warnings of shots being fired at fellow security officers.

After a while, the cruiser seemed to pick up speed. He could feel it turn occasionally without slowing down. Not once since they hid inside did the officer respond to any calls. He just kept driving.

Glancing over at Nikki, he noticed a concerned expression on her face, which only heightened his anxiety.

She attempted to smile at him, but she must also have thought it was unconvincing as it faded quickly. Resting his head against the back of the driver's seat, Sebastian closed his eyes, trying to find the courage to face whatever was going to happen when the cruiser finally came to a halt.

The screeching of tires and blaring of horns pulled him from his trance. Forcefully pressed against the front seats as the officer slammed on his breaks, Sebastian and Nikki were thrown from their hiding places when the cruiser was suddenly struck near the front driver's side. Shards of glass sprayed over them, cutting Sebastian just above his left eyebrow. Feeling blood dripping down his face, he reached up. Drawing his hand away, he found his fingertips stained red.

The rear driver's side door was being forced open, and Sebastian felt his body dragged out from the backseat, for a split second reliving the nightmarish memory of the accident years ago when he was abducted. Closing his eyes, he winced as the pain radiated from his back and head. While he lay on the ground fighting for breath, he heard people yelling over the sounds of sirens in the distance. Although dazed, he thought her heard Nikki calling his name, but couldn't be sure of this.

***

Glancing up, his eyes fixed on the cell bars, Lee listened to the sounds of someone approaching, already knowing who it was by the echoes of her shoes tapping against the concrete floor. Stepping into view, Lydia stared at the three of them before focusing only on her father. "Hello, Daddy," she uttered with her usual relaxed lilt in her voice. "I have something here for you, rather bad news, I'm afraid." Reaching her hand through the bars, she held out an electronic tablet for her father to take.

Reluctantly rising from his cot, Lee slowly wandered over to her, with Abdul and Scotty flanking him.

As he took the tablet from her, Lydia continued, "This film footage was taken by a security camera in Chinatown about an hour ago. I assure you of its authenticity."

Looking at the screen, Lee touched the arrow, allowing the video image to play. For a moment, nothing appeared until a black security cruiser instantly drove into view. To their surprise, it was then broadsided on the front driver's side by a silver pickup truck. Continuing to watch, he saw several people rush over to the cruiser, forcing open the driver's side front and rear doors and dragging two people out from the seats. At first, everything was obscured by several people crowding around the driver, beating him until his head exploded with a shower of sparks erupting from his internal robotics. The camera then zoomed in on the person lying on the ground. Lee's hands quaked in recognition of Sebastian's bloodied face. A Chinese girl, kneeling down next to him, seemed frantic in begging for help while trying to revive him. Shaking his head, Lee angrily stared as Lydia. "This is a lie," his tone a harsh rasp. "Somehow you've found a way to impose his image into this footage."

Casual with her response, Lydia answered, "As I said before, the footage is authentic, completely tamperproof—as designed by Dryden Technologies. Wouldn't you agree, Scotty? Seeing Nikki, *alone*, should confirm this."

Quickly glancing to Scotty, Lee asked, "You *know* that girl?"

Looking closer at the screen, Scotty nodded his head. "Yeah, that's her. I'm sure of it. I sent her a text message before we were arrested, asking for her help." With his eyes wet with tears, he looked directly at Lee. "That's *her*—and—I think that's *him*—and I think—that you know it's him, too."

"The coroner signed his death certificate about a half hour ago," Lydia flatly confirmed. "If you'd like, I could bring you a copy?"

Wanting desperately to throw the tablet against the wall, Abdul grabbed it from him before he could damage it. Closing his eyes, counting rapidly to ten to calm his anger, Lee sighed deeply as he looked at Scotty and Abdul. Stepping away from the cell door, Lee firmly placed his hands on Scotty's shoulders, their eyes fixed on each other's. Barely holding his own emotions in, Lee uttered, "Not until I hold his body in my arms—will I ever believe that my son is dead."

"That can be arranged," Lydia interrupted. "All you have to do is say *please*."

"Go to hell!" Lee bellowed at her, banging his fists against the cell wall until Abdul pulled him away, silently attempting to soothe him while restraining his arms.

"Let me know if you change your mind," Lydia offered as she walked away.

"*Damn her*," Lee whispered, closing his eyes for a moment while resting his forehead against the cell door. When he opened them again, he noticed Lexia standing there in her cell, staring at him. "I imagine you enjoyed the show," he mumbled to her.

Forcing out a laugh, Lexia replied, "I was a *captive* audience." Leaning her head back against the wall, she sighed heavily as she blankly gazed forward. "You know if I thought I could have gotten away with it, I would have killed you years ago."

"What makes you think you wouldn't have got away with it?"

Turning her face toward him, she answered, "Killing *you* would have been easy. You were never really alive after Lydia arranged your son's abduction. I could have made your death look like a suicide, a distraught father overwhelmed by the loss of his precious child."

"Why didn't you?"

Drawing her glance away from him, Lexia whispered, "Because Lydia was always watching, always observing even the smallest of details, a trait she inherited from you. She would have figured everything out. And then—I imagine she would have blackmailed me—or worse."

"So—why didn't you just kill *her*?"

Crookedly smiling, Lexia responded, "Who said I didn't?"

Chapter Fourteen

Sitting quietly with his knees pulled up to his chin, Scotty listened to a faintly whispered conversation between his dad and Lee.

"Do you believe the Lydia *here*—is, in fact, a replicate?" Abdul asked.

Sighing, Lee responded, "It's possible. If I could only get her to step closer, I could reach out and bash her skull against the metal bars."

"And your wife; is she capable of committing the murder of your daughter?"

"Don't call Lydia that. She stopped being my daughter a long time ago. As for Lexia, yes, I think we both know she's capable of murder."

"Yes," Abdul agreed.

Muffling a sob, Lee attempted to compose himself as Abdul comfortingly rested his hand on his shoulder. "You can't believe what she said about Sebastian. You know she's lying."

"No, my friend, I don't know that. If she is, in fact, a replicate—then she's telling the truth." Brushing away his tears, Lee continued, "I've watched the development of replicates since their first designs were revealed. They can be programmed to hate, kill, and inflict punishment. And a replicate is completely incapable of telling lies. They can only speak the truth as has been presented to them."

"There you have it! Only the truth *as has been presented to them*. Lydia has been programmed with what she believes is the truth. The camera footage she provided clearly shows him injured—but does not confirm that he died. As for her remarks about the death certificate, that is a document that can easily be forged."

Pounding his palm against his forehead, Lee uttered, "My mind clearly understands everything you've said—but my heart isn't so convinced."

"Have faith, my friend. For twelve years, Sebastian was missing—yet somehow found his way back to you. Don't give up on him so quickly."

"How very—*touching*," Lexia rudely chimed in from her dark corner.

Exhaling away his own concerns for Sebastian, Scotty traced his finger across the top of the tablet, unexpectedly turning it on. After spending only a few minutes randomly typing in words, Scotty found the correct password, turning on the tablet left by Lydia. "*Yes!*" he exclaimed as he gained access to social media sites.

Wandering over to him, Both Abdul and Lee sat on opposite sides of him, watching with curiosity. "What are you doing?" his dad asked.

"You'll never believe this—but we have complete internet access."

"Pull up the national news," Lee requested.

Appearing on-screen was a live streaming newsfeed from Washington D.C. Sitting at a desk surrounded by numerous monitors, the newscaster began updating viewers with national headlines. "As the fallout from the leaked Nightfall data continues to cause havoc both nationally and internationally, the President is only minutes away from addressing an emergency meeting of foreign ministers at the temporary headquarters of the United Nations in Paris. We will be joining our chief foreign correspondent shortly.

Here at home order has been restored in most major cities with the exceptions of New York and San Francisco. The extensive amount of arrests for synthetic replicates in New York has reached epidemic proportions with an estimated five thousand public officials, Wall Street executives, and prominent members of political parties being detained. Widespread corruption and rampant security issues have forced many to flee as anti-government demonstrations continue to turn violent.

As for San Francisco, the tense situation there continues to deteriorate as protestors, both joined and backed by the former police force continue to clash with the city's private security force, accused of being manned with synthetic replicates. California's governor has indicated that should San Francisco's mayor not disband his private security force immediately, then the National Guard will take further steps to curtail the violence, up to and including a full-scale invasion of the city."

"Do you think Dad is okay?" Scotty asked, glancing cautiously at Abdul.

"I hope so," he quietly responded.

"Do you—ever think—you could forgive him for what he did?"

With the saddest of smiles, Abdul chokingly answered, "I—already—have. That's what you do when you love someone."

Returning their attention to the screen, an image of a large packed gallery appeared with the President walking up to a podium. Nodding his head to several people in the hushed crowd, he tapped his finger on the microphone and then began his speech. "Esteemed ladies and gentlemen, by speaking here before you today, it is my hope to impress upon you the continuing vigilance I have in eradicating the synthetic replicate threat both in the United States and across the globe. Public outcry over this plot initiated by my predecessor in collusion with corporate entities has not fallen on deaf ears. Please allow me to assure you that—"

All three of their eyes burst wide as the President's head exploded with showering sparks from an assailant's gunshot, revealing his robotic brain before severely convulsing and falling to the ground. The picture on the screen quickly returned to the newscaster in Washington sitting at his desk visibly stunned and unable to speak.

"Did you see what I just saw?" Scotty uttered.

Lee, resting his face in the palms of his hands, offered nothing while Abdul breathlessly mumbled, "This is beyond—anything imaginable."

Thinking fast, Scotty minimized the image on the screen as he connected the tablet with a social media site.

"What are you doing?" Abdul asked.

"I'm trying to send a message to Nikki, but—"

"But what?" Lee interrupted.

Shaking his head while still looking at the screen, Scotty answered, "Doesn't all this seem too easy? It's as if––"

"She wanted us to see everything," Abdul finished his son's sentence. "But more than that—"

"She wants us to keep using the tablet," Lee interrupted. "She's probably tracking everything you're doing as we speak," he guessed. "Lydia knew I wouldn't believe her lie about my son's death—and the only way she can find him is by you contacting Nikki."

"I'm not sure of how much of a chance they have to survive if I don't." Scotty continued, "Nikki doesn't know where to go. And if Sebastian *is* hurt—then he may not be able to tell her where they need to go if he hasn't already."

Looking to Lee, Abdul added, "It's a risk we have no choice but to take."

Placing his hand on Scotty's shoulder, Lee whispered, "Send her the message."

***

Breathing deep, Sebastian inhaled a pungent aroma reeking from a mixture of spices and something else he couldn't recognize. Swallowing hard, the throbbing just above his eye caused him feelings of light-headedness and nauseous. Blinking his eyes open, his watery vision prevented him from focusing on a shadow continuously passing in front of his eyes. "Where am I?" he faintly uttered.

Feeling someone squeeze his hand, Sebastian heard Nikki's voice. "We're in Chinatown. We're safe."

"What's happening to me?"

"The gash above your eye is getting stitched."

"Are we in a hospital?"

"No. We're in a small fabrics shop. The seamstress is stitching you up."

"How did we get here?"

"Her sons pulled you off the street. They're helping us hide from the security forces."

"What is that smell?"

"A spicy dinner—and opium." Giggling, Nikki revealed, "I'm getting a serious buzz off this stuff. She's burning it so you don't feel the stitches. Do you feel them?"

"No—but that stuff is making me sick."

Catching another whiff of the opium's stench, it seemed less fragrant after a moment, as if it had been taken away.

Glancing over at her, Sebastian noticed a pleasant expression on her pretty face. He held his breath as she leaned down, brushing her lips against his before kissing him. "What was that for?" he quietly asked.

Laughing as she smiled, Nikki answered, "Let's just say I have a thing for your soft gray eyes."

Feeling butterflies in his stomach, his pulse was now racing. Sebastian commented, "You know—I have two." Smiling even bigger, Nikki leaned down, kissing him much longer this time.

Pulling her head back, her eyes glanced down, seeing the tremor coursing through his hand. Gently holding it, she whispered, "You can relax for a little while."

Understanding she thought his tremor was caused by fear, Sebastian wondered how to tell her about his

Parkinson's disease. However, the unexpected vibrations of her cell phone disrupted their sweet moment.

"It's a message from Scotty! But—all it sent—is an address, 24 South Meridian Drive. I wonder if this is where they're being held?" she hopefully questioned.

"I don't think so," Sebastian answered. "That's where he lives. Why would they be holding him there?"

* * *

Running his baton across the cell bars, the guard yelled, "*Dryden*! It's time." Rubbing his eyes, Lee glanced warily toward the cell door, seeing three guards and Lydia standing there waiting for him.

"It's time, Daddy," Lydia echoed the guard's words with her usual relaxed smirk.

Abdul's hand grasped Lee's arm as he was rising from his cot. Both, at a loss for words to say, nodded their heads, exchanging smiles brimming with sadness as Lee pulled away. Looking over to Scotty, he silently mouthed the words, 'thank you', as he stepped over to the now open door.

Lexia remained silent in her cell, not drawing attention to herself in the dark corner. Lee thought he should say something to her, yet nothing worth the effort came to mind. He knew how ecstatic she was probably feeling and forbid himself from offering her the satisfaction of any final words uttered from him.

Now staring at Lydia, wondering if this was in fact, her or a replicate, he neither felt anger toward her nor fear of what would come next. What Lexia had said was the truth. Having watched his beloved Melinda die in the car crash and seeing his son taken away from him, he had led the life of a dead man from that terrible moment on. Yet seeing his son again and spending precious time with him in the Daybreak were moments or resurrection, moments he intended to focus on as his final minutes of life dwindled away. "I'm ready," Lee whispered with Lydia offering no response. "Aren't you going to cuff me?"

As usual, Lydia brushed off answering the question. With his baton, the first guard motioned in the direction he wanted Lee to walk. The sensation of the cool concrete under his bare feet caused Lee to shiver. And maybe it simply was the adrenaline coursing through him, anticipating what he knew came next.

Walking through the dimly lit hallway leading to a bright light behind the twin doors, he swallowed deeply, feeling no moisture in his throat. With his heart pounding and his pulse racing, he nervously exhaled when the doors automatically opened. Stepping inside what appeared to be an operating room, he inhaled the air's sterility. Lee felt his legs grow weak when he saw a body covered by a white sheet lying on a gurney next to the one he believed was meant for him.

"I had your son brought here so you could say good-bye to him," Lydia offered.

"That's not my son," he faked calmness he didn't feel as he responded. "Probably—a synthetic replicate— just like you." Glancing away toward a large window showing a dozen unoccupied chairs on the other side, as well as a surveillance camera, Lee quietly commented, rather than asking, "I imagine the guests will be arriving soon—for my going away party."

"One is already here," Lydia revealed.

Watching the door open, Lee's jaw dropped stunned by the presence of an unexpected guest, although one he should have anticipated.

Chapter Fifteen

Walking over to the cell bars, Scotty pressed his head against them, feeling the coolness of the steel. He shook the bars to release his pent-up frustration. From the corner of his eye he spied the unbelievable—a slight movement of the cell door. He sidestepped over and wrapped his fingers around two of the bars. Pushing lightly against the heavy door, it offered no resistance as it moved. With increased force, he kept pushing until the door fully opened. "Dad, you gotta see this," he mumbled.

Opening his tear-soaked eyes, Abdul clearly stunned by the unlocked door, stumbled from his cot. "What-is-this-devilry?" he choked out.

"It's an open door," Scotty answered. "We could debate the why of it being open—or we could leave," he added.

"Do you believe this open door leads to freedom?" Abdul asked, placing his hands on his son's shoulders.

"No. You taught me better than that."

"Good man," Abdul commended him. "So—where does this lead?"

Looking at his dad, Scotty whispered, "Let's find out." Nodding his approval, they treaded lightly out into the hallway after checking both directions for any signs of the guards. Pointing in the direction Lee had been led away to, Scotty watched his dad shake his head no, motioning for them to head in the opposite direction. Hearing a sound coming from where he wanted to go, Scotty realized why his dad was refusing to go the way he was headed.

Sneaking to the end of the hallway, Scotty peered around the left corner, finding one of the guards smoking, leaning against the wall with his back to him. Wandering over, Scotty stood next to him, casually asking, "How's it goin'?" Leaning closer to the startled guard, Scotty added, "Did you know some of the prisoners escaped?" Before the guard could react, Abdul had wrapped his arm around his neck, dragging him down to the ground in a choke hold. He struggled for only a moment before passing out.

"Take his baton, keys, and flashlight," Abdul whispered. Scotty did as he was told.

"What are we going to do with him?"

Noticing another set of doors further down the hallway, Abdul grabbed the guard by his ankles, pulling him across the floor to the doors. Thinking it was a storage room, both Scotty and Abdul jumped in surprise when they heard voices coming from the darkness within. Pushing the door in, both saw another guard sitting at a desk lit by a small desk lamp and his computer screen. "About time you get off break," the guard uttered with disgust without turning around. Once more hearing voices, he bellowed out, "Quiet! You'd think you could follow an order—" Bashing the baton against the guard's skull, Abdul halted him from finishing his sentence as he fell unconscious across the desk.

Pushing him off his seat, Scotty sat down, reading the information on the screen while Abdul wandered slightly away. "Dad, you're not going to believe this. There must be hundreds of pictures of synthetic replicates—that the government—plans to—*reprogram*. They're telling everyone that the robots are being destroyed—when in fact—they intend—to unleash them back into society."

"You should see this," Abdul said to Scotty pointing the flashlight into the darkness.

Slowly walking over to his dad, Scotty's eyes grew large as he watched what the flashlight's bright beam revealed. From one cell to the next, people crowded up to the bars, blankly staring out in clear fascination at the light.

Moving further into the darkness, Abdul pointed the light both left and right on this level, as well as directing the beam to the upper level, revealing even more people. Softly spoken murmurs among them suggested the obvious. "Dad, these—aren't people, are they? They're replicates."

"Hundreds of them," Abdul confirmed. The eeriness of the darkened cell block intensified as the treaded further down to the end. Scotty smelled a salty dampness in the air, prompting the question, "Where do you think we are?"

Waving the flashlight beam in different directions, Abdul answered, "Alcatraz. I recognize this cell block from a television show I once saw."

"What kind of show?" Scotty nervously asked.

"About haunted places."

Before Scotty could say anything else, a woman near them began screaming. Her blood-chilling wails loudly echoed, forcing Scotty and Abdul to cover their ears. Using the flashlight to find the woman, Abdul finally caught glimpse of her in one of the center cells. Walking up to the bars, he reached in, seizing the woman by the back of her neck. Forcing her head to collide with the bars—after twice impacting her skull against the cold steel, her facial mask fractured with smoke rising from underneath, silencing her cries of terror.

"Why was she doing that?" Scotty frantically asked.

"Possibly a malfunction. She must have suffered internal damage while being brought here."

"A correct assumption," a deep male voice one cell over responded.

"Who said that?" Scotty called out.

"I did," the voice answered.

"And—who is *I*?" Abdul questioned.

Flashing the light into the cell, they noticed someone moving through the overcrowded space up to the door. "That would be me," an older, black man offered, pleasantly adding, "My name is Maurice Burns."

"And what is your current program?" Abdul inquired.

"Technical support for mobile devices. Consumers would call in with inquiries regarding account payment status to questions involving device malfunctions. With the latter, I would gain remote access to their Smartphones and such, resolving the technical issues while accessing their personal data for financial records or incriminating files such as anti-government posts and illicit pornography. I would then share this information with the security administration."

"And people never picked up on this," Scotty mumbled in disbelief.

"Never to my knowledge," Maurice responded. "Protocol dictated that when performing my function, my voice would be altered to a dialect of Asian-subcontinental origin, Pakistani or Indian, offering the consumer the impression they were dealing with a representative in a foreign country. Most consumers would be too exasperated in dealing with me to realize the breach of security they willingly allowed."

"Unbelievable," Scotty uttered.

"I assure you, my programming does not include the capability to lie."

"Why are you fully functional while all others around you appear to have their programs disabled," Abdul questioned.

"Human error."

Urging his dad to step away from the cell door, Scotty whispered, "Dad, I have a bad feeling about these replicates. What do you think the government intends to do with them?"

"I could provide the answer for you, as I have significant remote access to the data relating to my replicate peers," Maurice offered. "I possess security clearances which could easily reveal government plans."

Stepping back to the cell door, Abdul asked, "What are the government's intentions with these replicate?"

"Infiltration into society with the intended purpose of eliminating political obstacles both here and abroad."

"Dad, we have to stop this," Scotty mumbled.

"Indeed."

"How do we do it?"

"We need to destroy them."

"How?"

Once more interrupting, Maurice suggested, "The most obvious and thorough way would be to detonate the ammunitions discretely stored in the lower level. The resulting blast should bring the entire prison down, culminating with the destruction of all replicates, as well as the untimely deaths of any humans who remain on the island."

"I doubt we would survive by lighting a match and running," Scotty mumbled with sarcasm.

"That would be a rather barbaric approach," Maurice confirmed, adding, "highly doable—but inefficient with numerous variables that could lead to failure. If I may, a more practical approach of remotely setting one of the detonators, allowing for time to escape, would be a far more viable option in achieving your goal, to include your survival."

"Are you capable of completing such a task?" Abdul asked.

"Of course. All I require is access to a laptop computer."

Glancing down at the key ring, Scotty wondered aloud, "Which key opens the cell door?" Both his and his dad's jaws dropped when Maurice opened the door with ease, now realizing that it was never locked. "Can't the other replicates escape?"

"They lack the programming to do so," Maurice answered.

"This way," Abdul said, motioning for Maurice to follow him. Returning to the guard's desk, Maurice sat down and quickly began typing on the keyboard. After several minutes he looked up from his work, asking, "What time should the detonation be scheduled?"

Abdul answered, "Nine o'clock, as the sun goes down", noting the time on the computer screen closing in on six o'clock in the evening. "That should give us enough time to find our friend and a boat to escape the island."

"I'll send a text message to Nikki, telling her where we're at and to bring Sebastian with her," he said, looking to his dad with hope in his eyes that his friend was still alive. Abdul nodded his approval.

Returning his stare to the computer screen, Maurice asked, "Are you referring to Lee Dryden?"

"Yes."

Reading from information appearing on the screen, Maurice confirmed, "His execution by lethal injection is scheduled to begin at this very moment."

***

Lee watched as each seat in the viewing gallery was claimed by individuals he'd never met before. "Who are they?"

Uncharacteristic for her, Lydia matter-of-factly answered, "Government officials. I would have invited your brother in Nebraska—but there wasn't enough time for him to make it here. I also thought of inviting a member of the clergy. However, not knowing which religion you would be comfortable with, I chose not to offer an invitation, should you have found offense if I selected incorrectly."

Emerging from the private viewing gallery opposite the one occupied by the invited guests, Lydia strolled over to Lee Dryden, who lay on the gurney next to the body of his son. "Would you like to offer any final words?"

Staring out toward the filled gallery of witnesses, he said nothing.

"Please proceed," Lydia instructed the attending medical staff. Returning to her vantage point behind a glass window hiding her from public view, she said to the guest, "The drugs take roughly ten minutes through the intravenous tube before reaching the heart. You should die shortly after that."

"You mean my *replicate* should die," Lee corrected her, for which she offered no response. Resting his head against the window as he watched his robotic twin being injected with poison through a clear tube, he wondered aloud, "So why go to all this trouble? The government will be satisfied that I'm dead, no longer a threat to further expose their diabolical plans. But—*you*—need me alive for something else, something the replicate you created of me can't provide." Lydia's cunning smirk confirmed this.

Chapter Sixteen

"You look tired," Nikki commented, tracing the back of her hand against Sebastian's cheek.

"I am tired. I feel like I want to pass out."

"You just need some rest. Once we get to Scotty's house, maybe you can take a nap. We should get going." The unexpected buzzing of Nikki's cell phone startled them both as Sebastian sat up. "It's another text message from Scotty," she burst out. Reading it aloud, she seemed confused. "Forget my last message. We are at Alcatraz. You and Sebastian need to come to the docks."

"Why are they on Alcatraz?" Sebastian wondered. "That place has been abandoned for decades."

"Until recently," Nikki corrected him. "I saw a report on the news about the government using it as a termination point for replicates." Noticing the tremors coursing through both his hands, she took hold of each, offering him a reassuring smile as she did. "Everything is going to be okay. We're going to find them and then get out of the city."

Unable to hold back, Sebastian blurted out, "I have Parkinson's disease." With her eyes large as saucers, her smile quickly fading, he added, "That's why my hands are shaking. That's why I'm so tired—and feel light-headed."

"I don't understand," Nikki uttered. "I got a shot, protecting me from that disease years ago."

"I didn't," Sebastian confessed. "No one cared that much about me."

"I'm sorry," She said, kissing him softly on his cheek.

"It's okay. We should get going." At first when Sebastian stood, he wobbled a bit before gaining his balance. He turned to the old Chinese woman who had stitched his cut and her sons. "Thank you," he offered, bowing slightly to them.

"Yes, thank you," Nikki echoed. They bowed in turn to both of them as they left.

Stepping outside, Sebastian glanced up at the breathtaking orange sky, directly contrasting with the bland, run-down facades of the shops and homes in this part of the city. Bars covered the windows of shops still open while abandoned storefronts displayed rental and sale signs. One other thing, clearly noticeable when they stepped outside, was how quiet everything seemed. There was no one walking on the sidewalks or driving down the street that could be seen. Even the trash blown by the silent breezes withheld their sound. The entire neighborhood appeared as if it were a ghost town.

"Darn it!" Nikki mumbled with frustration, tapping on her cell phone.

"What's wrong?"

"Every time I try to send a text back to Scotty, it won't go through. I don't understand how he can send messages to me but I can't send messages back."

"Maybe his phone is broken. Maybe he can only send messages," Sebastian guessed.

"Maybe that's it. Come on, this way," Nikki motioned toward the street corner.

"Halt—or I will shoot," a deep stern voice sounded from behind them as they stopped in the center of the street. Fearfully turning around, Sebastian felt his pulse racing, staring into the damaged face of a replicate security guard, the same one they rode with into this section of town. With the continuous shifting of his gun from one direction to another, Sebastian quickly realized that the guard had been blinded, possibly by those who dragged him from the cruiser and repeatedly beat him. Sparks from one of his eye sockets erupted as his robotic body convulsed. "Halt—or—I—will—shoot," he said once more with slower words.

Lunging forward, the guard pressed the barrel of his gun harshly into Sebastian's forehead. Unable to control the quaking in his arms and legs, Sebastian held his breath and closed his eyes. He believed that his heart would explode through his chest. He was close to throwing up. Sebastian anxiously exhaled when Nikki whispered to him.

"I-want-you-to-slowly-back-away-from-the-guard. Trust me."

As a tear streamed down his cheek, Sebastian took one step back and then another.

"Halt—or—" Further words from the guard's voice sounded garbled to the point of being unintelligible. Backing up to a post office box positioned on the edge of the sidewalk, Sebastian held still, afraid to move. Blinking his eyes open, the rev of an engine echoed only a moment before a fast-moving delivery truck ran the security guard down, scattering his shattered robotic pieces across the street. Landing at his feet, pointing slightly to the left was the gun held by the security guard. Nervously glancing at it, the gun rapidly fired, the bullet ricocheting off the sidewalk, forcing Sebastian to fall against the post office box in fear. Nikki screamed and kicked it away before crouching down next to him.

With his chest heaving, fighting to catch his breath, he forced out from his throat. "*Did—you—*"

"Know the truck was coming?" Nikki finished his question. "Yeah, I saw it barreling toward us."

"I didn't," he answered, blankly staring out.

"You were probably too scared to hear it," Nikki reasoned. Helping him up, she pulled on his sleeve. "Come on, we gotta get going. The docks are a few blocks away."

***

Arriving at the docks, Sebastian's eyes were drawn to the fiery orange sky reflecting its brilliance off the water's surface, making the bay appear as an endless pool of scorching molten lava. "What now?" he uttered, searching each direction for ways to reach Alcatraz.

"I don't know," Nikki answered with a sigh.

Sebastian's heart began to race when at a distance he saw Xavier pacing back and forth. He heard Nikki shout out, "Where are you going?" as he ran over to him.

Xavier, appearing distressed to the point of shock, blankly stared at him as he approached. *"Where's—my—dad—and--Scotty—and—Abdul?"* Sebastian forced out, panting to catch his breath.

"I tried to protect them," Xavier faintly mumbled. "I—thought I could save them. They'll never forgive me. I tried to protect them."

"What are you talking about?"

Reaching them, Nikki cautiously glanced at Xavier. "What's wrong with him?"

"I don't know." Waving his hand in front of Xavier's eyes, noticing how his eyes failed to blink, Sebastian continued, "Something happened to him. He keeps saying he tried to protect them—and save them." Hoping to gain his attention, Sebastian placed his hands on Xavier's shoulders. "How do we get on the island? *Please*—I need your help," he begged.

Looking to his right, Xavier mumbled, "Only the dead go there."

"What does that mean?"

"I think I know," Nikki answered for Xavier. "Come on, this way," she said, dragging Sebastian away.

"What about Xavier?"

"We don't have time to worry about him. Come on!"

Not far down the docks, Sebastian and Nikki arrived at a warehouse surrounded by a chain-linked fence. Watching from a distance, they saw men unloading black body bags from a large white truck. "Look at all those dead people," he whispered.

"They're not people. They're replicated. When your friend mentioned the dead, I knew right away what he was talking about. I remembered seeing something online about damaged replicates being taken to storage facilities. Remember what I said about the government using Alcatraz as a termination point for replicates? I would bet anything that those replicates are being taken over to the island for disposal." Pointing at the body bags, Nikki added, "That's how we're going to get over to Alcatraz."

"How?"

"We're going to get inside those body bags and pretend to be broken replicates. That's our way onto the island. Look! The men are walking away. Come on!"

Sneaking through an unlocked gate, they quickly made their way to the closest body bags. Unzipping the first, both were startled to see what appeared to be a gang member with chains on his clothing and tattoos visible on his arms. Silently they pulled his riddled with bullet holes body from the bag, dragging him out of sight behind some large crates. Returning to the body bag, Nikki whispered, "Stuff yourself in this one. I'll get in the one over there."

"Are you sure about this?" Sebastian worriedly asked while struggling to get in.

"Yes," she answered confidently, dragging the zipper up to his chest. Leaning down, she kissed him and smiled. "For luck. I'll see you at Alcatraz." Pulling the zipper up, leaving enough of a slit for him to breathe through, Sebastian saw her wink at him before disappearing from his sight.

"Hey, you! Get away from there!" he heard a loud man's harsh voice shout. Hearing the sounds of running coming closer, Sebastian fearfully closed his eyes, expecting to be caught. His heart nearly stopped while holding his breath when he heard the man say, "What have we here? A thief."

"I was just curious," he overheard Nikki's attitude-filled answer.

"What should we do with her?" another man asked.

"Toss her butt out of here, that's what. If we catch you in here again, we won't be so nice, sweetheart," the first man warned. Sebastian heard the sounds of their shoes walking away. When all was quiet, he exhaled the breath he'd been holding, attempting to control the tremors shaking his body. The stifling heat inside the bag left him sweating and within minutes, he was breathing in the pungent smell from inside the plastic. A quickly passing thought crossed his mind, wondering if this was what it felt like to be thrown away like garbage.

Hearing approaching footsteps, Sebastian's moment of rest came to an abrupt halt as he felt his body being awkwardly lifted "What the…" escaping from his lips.

"What did you say?" one of the men asked.

"I didn't say anything," the other answered. "You're just being paranoid with all these bodies around."

"Let's just get them onto the boat and be done with it," the first man grumbled.

***

Emerging from a security door on the far side of the prison, Lydia led her father to a small, secluded dock with a motorboat tied to it for their escape. Halting his steps, Lee turned back to Lydia as she pointed her gun at him. "I'm not going any further until you answer some questions," Lee calmly demanded.

Maintaining the pleasant lilt in her voice, Lydia responded, "You are in no position to issue demands. I could kill you right now if you prefer."

"No you won't," he argued, adding, "You need me *alive*. Otherwise, I would have died from lethal injection back there in the operating room." Lydia maintained her silence as he continued, "Now—what would that be? Why do you want me alive?"

"I need your eyes," she revealed.

"Of course," Lee softly uttered, glancing away in thought. "You need my eyes for scanning so you can gain entry into by private lab at One Legacy Place." Expressing a knowing grin, he spoke on. "You think that by accessing my personal data and software—you'll be able to override the Nightfall command and stop the hemorrhaging of classified information onto the internet."

"Yes."

"You *thought* you could achieve this when you created a synthetic replicate of me. But—for some reason—you couldn't duplicate my eyes."

"Correct," Lydia confirmed. "Your eyes hold microscopic flecks of silver. Our technology is not advanced enough to recreate such a physical anomaly."

"And—what makes you think that I'll do what you want?"

"You *will*—if you hope to see your son alive."

Lee's eyes grew large before stating, "So you are capable of telling lies. I knew he wasn't dead."

"Yes," Lydia confessed. Before Lee could ask her where his son is, someone unexpected joined them.

"We seem to be in the habit of impromptu family gatherings," Lexia interrupted. As Lexia stepped closer, holding a gun in her hand, Lydia drew back, appearing slightly confused.

"Now look what you've done," Lee sarcastically scolded his wife. "You've overwhelmed her programming."

Quickly raising her hand, Lexia aimed the gun at Lydia's head, firing once. Following the explosion of sparks, the bullet's ricochet struck Lee on the shoulder, sending him staggering back off the dock, hearing Lexia yell his name. Plunging under the water's surface, he gazed up through the blood-tainted water at his wife's fluid image as he sank deeper and deeper.

Chapter Seventeen

Abdul and Scotty quietly passed down a brightly lit hallway leading to a makeshift medical ward. Approaching twin doors, Scotty stopped, his breathing growing rapid. "You should stay out here," his dad said, comfortingly touching his cheek. "There's no need for you to see this."

Swallowing deep, Scotty shook his head. "No, Dad, I need to go in there."

Sighing, Abdul whispered, "All right."

Parting the doors, Abdul led Scotty into what appeared to be a dimly lit surgical room. Inhaling the sterile air, Scotty shuddered with chills from the cold airflow seeping in through vents on the ceiling. At the room's center were two white body bags atop side-by-side gurneys. Slowly stepping over to the first, Abdul's hand slightly quaked when reaching for the zipper. Nervously exhaling, he pulled the zipper down just enough to reveal the person's face. As he lowered his head, he briefly closed his eyes, opening them again to look upon Lee's face. "I'm sorry, my friend," he uttered in a whispered tone.

Moving over to the second gurney, Scotty glided his fingers across the surface of the body bag, attempting to summon the courage to reveal who lay inside. Anxiously shifting his weight from one side to the other, his fingertips touched the zipper without pulling it down. His dad's hand covered his, tenderly massaging his skin. "You don't have to do this," he heard his dad say.

"Yes, yes I do," he answered, barely loud enough to hear.

Together they pulled the zipper down, exposing Sebastian's face. For a moment Scotty stood there paralyzed by what he saw. Wrapping his son in his strong embrace, Abdul waited silently for Scotty to fall apart and held him closer when he did. With his tears falling onto Sebastian's face, every word he wanted to say remained deep in his throat, finding no strength to force them out.

Dragging him away, Abdul murmured in Scotty's ear, "They're together again. I promise." Looking into his son's tear-soaked face, he added, "We need to go." Kissing Scotty's forehead, Abdul led him away through the twin doors. Following a path that Maurice had provided them with instructions for, they soon reached a ferry about to depart for San Francisco. Sneaking aboard, they found a quiet spot where they sat watching as the ferry floated away from the dock. Only once during the trip to the city did either of them take their eyes off Alcatraz.

***

Sebastian placed his hand firmly over his mouth, nauseated by motion sickness from the boat he believed he was on. His back ached from being slammed down hard over what he thought might be another body under his. Feeling pressed from both sides, the heat inside the body bag had his jacket clinging to his sweat-soaked frame. And through the open slit, he heard the incessant calls of seagulls as he watched the sky growing darker.

After what seemed like an endless amount of time, he once more heard the men's voices.

"What are you doing? Why are we stopping?"

"They're not paying me overtime, so we're going to dump the bodies here," another man answered.

"Sounds good to me," the first man said with a laugh. "They'll never miss 'em."

Panicked by what he overheard, Sebastian's mind rapidly thought of how to escape. Wanting to pry the zipper open to slip out of the body bag, it only moved an inch before it jammed. Feeling light-headed, gasping for air, he was seized with fear when the bottom of the bag was lifted into the air, followed by a forceful grasp near his head. Flailing vigorously, he tried wrenching the bag from their grips. "This one's not as damaged as the rest of them are," one of the men strained to utter. His breath rushed from his lungs, feeling weightless for only a moment.

Splashing water doused Sebastian's face when his body bag struck the water's surface. For only a moment, it seemed to float before he felt a pulling sensation from under him. The light penetrating through the open slit faded as water began seeping in. Realizing how little air he had left, Sebastian took a deep breath, frantically pulling at the zipper to free him. With each inch he forced, more and more of his body grew drenched. A rush of bubbles from his nostrils clouded his view of the surface, appearing much dimmer.

With one final yank, the zipper separated enough for Sebastian to free his head and shoulders from the bag. Glancing out through the light murky water, he saw body bags descending into the bay's shadowy depths. From one such bag, he watched a hand reach out and noticed what he thought might be sparks, quickly extinguished. Kicking with his remaining strength, he forced the release of his legs from the bag, yet still felt his body being dragged deeper into the bay. Tugging at his jacket, he pulled it off, watching it float away from him. Swimming up, he expelled the last of his held breath just before breaching the surface.

Floating face up in the water, his eyes gazed upon the violet hues of the sky and a single star only moments revealed before sunset. Tremors coursed through him as small waves rushed over his heaving chest and shuddering legs. Spitting out water, he inhaled the salty air, silently wondering how he found the courage to survive the ordeal he had just lived through. Having no energy left, he felt himself drifting away, unable to even look around for any signs of help. Growing drowsy, Sebastian closed his eyes as the sounds of seagulls entranced him.

***

The return to San Francisco seemed endless with the sight of men dropping dead bodies into the water making the trip so much more terrible. Abdul and Scotty waited until all others aboard the ferry had left. Attempting to leave unnoticed, both were startled when they saw Maurice standing on the dock, watching seagulls flying overhead. Approaching him, Abdul commented, "I'm surprised you left Alcatraz without being programmed to do so."

Maurice responded in a matter-of-fact tone, "Self-destruct is not a component of my protocol."

Grinning from his answer, Abdul asked, "So what will you do now?"

Continuing to stare ahead, Maurice answered, "I will return to my apartment and sit at my desk, waiting for calls from consumers in need of answers for their questions."

"I may be one of those callers, someday," Abdul said, placing his hand on Maurice's shoulder.

"I remotely added my customer service cell phone number to your son's acquaintance directory should you find the need for future assistance. I will look forward to your call. Have a nice day." He then walked away, heading toward the city.

Turning in the opposite direction, Scotty was the first to see Xavier standing at a distance, watching them. Leaving Abdul behind, Scotty rushed up to Xavier, who at first appeared startled when his son embraced him. Bursting into tears, he held his son close, repeatedly mumbling, "I'm sorry, I'm sorry."

Abdul's approach to Xavier was much slower. With Scotty stepping to the side, Xavier brushed his tears away, attempting to compose himself. Once standing before each other, Xavier quaveringly begged, "Please forgive me. I love you. All I wanted—was to protect you."

"I know," Abdul quietly responded without moving closer.

Hesitantly taking a step forward, Xavier held out his hand. At first, Abdul resisted reaching out, but after a moment, he did, lightly tracing his fingers over Xavier's. Crying again, Xavier tried to smile. His breath seemed to rush out of him as Abdul drew closer to him. "Forgive me, *please*," he begged once more. Remaining silent, Abdul pulled Xavier into his arms, gently running his hand across his back as he fell apart, sobbing uncontrollably.

A grin split Scotty's face when he saw Nikki running toward him. "Scotty, we need to get over to Alcatraz—now!" she called out to him.

Looking at the time on the tablet he carried with him, he answered, "We can't. The place is set to explode in three minutes."

"No!" Nikki yelled. "Sebastian is being taken over there."

"Sebastian is dead," Scotty revealed. "We found his body an hour ago, along with his dad's."

"*That's—not—possible*," Nikki uttered. "He left here on a boat just over a half hour ago."

"What?" Abdul exclaimed.

"We were trying to sneak onto Alcatraz to look for you and his dad. He was inside a black body bag. Before I could climb in one, too, some men caught me and forced me to leave."

"A black body bag?" Abdul echoed her words. Looking at Scotty, both seemed to realize at the same time that Sebastian might have been in one of the bags tossed overboard from that boat their ferry passed. Running his hand across his beard in frustration, he saw the devastation so clear written in Scotty's expression. A moment later it was replaced by doubt.

"Dad, do you think—"

"That the bodies we saw—were replicates?" he finished Scotty's question.

Before he could answer, a thunderous detonation rattled the docks, each of them staggering from the intensity. Looking out over the bay, the dark waters were lit by the reflections of flames shooting through billowing plumes of smoke where Alcatraz once was. Sea-driven gusts of air, heated by the inferno, scorched their skin as large pieces of debris exploded against the water's surface. Dropping to his knees, Scotty watched the blaze rage with Nikki kneeling at his side. "Do you think there's a chance he didn't make it to the island?"

"Maybe. I don't know what to think," Scotty mumbled, continuing to stare out at the flames.

Chapter Eighteen

Two days later

After placing his backpack on the front passenger seat of Abdul's SUV, Scotty looked out toward the orange-pinkish hues of the morning sky. For a moment, he wondered what the same sky would look like far away from here. Seeing Abdul step out of the house pulled him from this thought.

Handing him a spray bottle and paper towels, Abdul grinned at him. "Would you clean the dust off the windshield?"

"Sure," Scotty said, in a distracted voice. "Are they going to be ready to leave soon?"

"I think so," his dad answered. "Nikki is fixing her hair and your dad is packing our lunch."

Looking up from wiping the window clean, Scotty hesitated, "Are you two okay? I mean, well—you know what I mean."

Sighing, Abdul smiled, responding, "We're better." Scotty nodded, feeling a little less anxious than before. "Come on. Let's try to motivate them so we can leave."

"How long do you think it will take to get to Alaska?"

Abdul was thoughtful for a moment before answering, "Two or three days, depending on how quickly we are allowed into Canada. They're screening refugees—"

"To make sure they're not replicates," Scotty finished his dad's sentence.

"Yes."

About ten minutes later, all four stepped out of the house, Xavier turned back to look one last time at their home. Taking hold of his hand, Abdul smiled at him. Releasing a deep breath, Xavier walked to the car, trying to grin, which seemed unconvincing.

"I thought I asked you to clean the windshield?" Abdul asked, pointing toward Scotty's side.

"I *did*," he answered confused. Reaching out, his fingers brushed some of the larger pieces of dirt into the palm of his hand. Closely observing, he glanced over to Abdul, grinning as he revealed, "This *isn't* dirt. It's— crumbs." After brushing the rest of the crumbs off the windshield, Scotty was about to get in when he found something next to his backpack. Reaching through the open window, he retrieved a book left for him, silently reading the title, *Brave New World*. "Thank you, my friend," he whispered, holding it close to him, exhilarated knowing Sebastian was alive.

Looking at Abdul, Scotty asked, "Do you think he'll be okay?"

"I hope so," his dad answered, smiling.

After fastening their seatbelts, Abdul touched a screen on the dashboard and requested. "What does the forecast show for today?"

A man's voice answered, "A low-pressure system is moving into the Pacific Northwest this evening with severe storms expected along the coast. Travel delays may occur from Portland to Seattle."

"Thank you, Maurice."

"You're welcome, sir. Have a nice day."

"Why do you call your satellite link, Maurice?" Nikki curiously asked from the backseat.

"No particular reason," Abdul answered, glancing at Scotty, exchanging sly grins.

***

Two weeks later

Arriving at the center of a small Maine seaside town, an old silver pickup truck stopped on the side of the road. Hopping out from the bed with his backpack, Sebastian peered into the front seat. "Thanks!" The driver nodded his head before driving away.

Glancing around, Sebastian read some of the storefront signs down Welsh Cove's picturesque tree-lined main street, smiling at the name on the barbershop, *Running with Scissors*. Antique and thrift shops were interspersed with a small post office, a bakery, and library, which he would have like to enter but was closed for the rest of the day according to the sign in the window

Walking by one display window after the next, he marveled at the unique items for sale, from toys to gadgets to decorative glassware. And he noticed how relaxed the people seemed, showing no signs of hostility and aggression as he'd witnessed when passing through places like Denver and Chicago. To him, it felt as if the clock had somehow turned back to a more innocent time before the replicate upheaval brought the country to a standstill.

He wandered over to the flagpole, gazing up at what someone had called *Old Glory*. This once proud symbol of unity still waved in the breeze over a land divided. He'd read that the New England states were planning a vote to secede, following the leads of Alaska and Texas. The new President holds hope that America will survive the replicate crisis, a view not shared by many, especially those in war zones such as New York and San Francisco.

Sitting down on a bench, Sebastian closed his eyes for a minute, feeling exhausted from the long trek across the country. He couldn't remember the last time he'd slept well, even thinking of the rides he'd been given and the train cars he'd hidden inside of. He noticed the tremors in both hands, appearing like they were getting worse along with feeling new aches in his muscles. But he'd come too far to let his deteriorating health stop him. When he stood up, everything began spinning for a minute as he steadied himself by gripping the handle on the bench. After regaining his balance, Sebastian began what he'd been told would be a short walk out of town to the place he'd traveled so far to see.

***

Massaging his sore shoulder, Lee blankly glanced out at the rolling waves crashing in on the shore as dusk approached. Robust sea-driven gales blew his hair back with the surf's echo slightly deafening him. Turning his eyes in the direction of the lighthouse, he deeply exhaled, content with finding refuge here yet more alone than he'd ever felt before.

Spying a fishing trawler out in the distance reminded him of the fisherman who'd pulled him out of the bay, back in San Francisco. He remembered how kind the old man was, taking great care to keep him as comfortable as possible when returning to port. Lee had told him that his sailboat had been boarded by thieves and that he'd been robbed and shot before being push overboard, a lie the old man believed.

After having his gunshot wound treated in one of the hospitals, Lee snuck away from the emergency room, finding a taxi that took him all the way to his home in Silicon Valley. From there, he escaped in an old corvette for the cross-country trip that brought him here, the one place reminding him of the two he loved most, his wife and son.

"*Dad*!" a voice called out up the beach from him. Lee staggered back, surprised and bewildered, watching his son running up to him. "Dad," his son said again. Staring intently at him, he believed he was seeing a ghost until he reached out, taking hold of his son's hand, feeling his flesh.

Stumbling back in confusion, Lee disbelievingly uttered, "How did you find this place?"

With eyes of full of wonder, his son answered, "It's just like I remembered it from the Daybreak, you, me, and mom."

"You remember her?" Lee uttered.

"Everything about her, Dad."

Covering his face with the palms of his hands, Lee released a sob and then wiped away his tears. Reaching behind his back, he pulled out a small handgun, pointing it at his son's head and pulling the trigger. An explosion of sparks instantly burst through the shattered remains of the replicate's facial mask as it dropped to its knees, falling forward onto the wet sand. Lee covered his nose, not wanting to breathe in the pungent stench of smoke rising from the robotic corpse.

***

With the straps from his backpack slipping from his grasp, Sebastian stood paralyzed several feet behind his dad. With his chest heaving and his pulse racing from fear, he swallowed hard, trying to force out words choked in his throat. Growing light-headed, he dropped to his knees with white seafoam washing over his legs, soaking his jeans.

Spinning around, his dad pointed the gun at him, shouting, "Who are you?"

Sebastian remained silent, closing his eyes, expecting to be shot.

"How did you find this place?" his dad's voice called out.

With his mind racing with thoughts he couldn't grasp, Sebastian somehow remembered something he'd seen inside the house. And with trembling words, he uttered, "I—w-was—guided—b-by—the light—of—t-the—nearest—star."

His body shuddered when hearing the click from the tripper. Wincing in anticipation of the bullet's impact with his skull, Sebastian's heart stopped with the air rushing from his lungs, as his dad's strong arms wrapping around him startled him. Sobbing uncontrollably, he heard his dad mumble, "I'm sorry. *Please*, I'm sorry."

***

Gazing up at the endless array of stars, Sebastian's eyes followed numerous meteors falling to Earth as if they were tears streaking across the midnight sky. He also watched the continuing motion of the beacon's light, flashing out to the dark ocean. The coolness of the night sea breezes sent chills through his body, as his feet dangled off the lighthouse observation deck and his bare chest rested up against the cold steel railing.

"I thought I might find you up here, kiddo," he was startled to hear his dad say from behind him. Easing down at his side, his dad draped a blanket around them both, pulling Sebastian closer to him. "You look tired."

"I am," Sebastian confessed. "I just don't want to fall asleep. I guess I'm afraid—"

"That I won't be here when you wake up," Lee finished his sentence.

"Yeah."

"I'm so sorry about what happened, about everything you went through."

"I don't blame you." After a quiet moment passed, Sebastian asked, "It was all Lydia's fault, wasn't it?"

"For the most part." His confusion with his dad's answer must have been apparent, causing his dad to further explain. "She was a victim like the rest of us."

"How?"

Sighing, Lee revealed, "Three years after Lydia was born, we found out that she had autism. She was always kind of different, not it a bad way. But there were things that troubled us, causing us to seek answers. Anyway, finding out gave us some perspective—but it didn't change how I felt about her. It was the same way I felt about you. When I held you both for the first time, my life changed. You both were the best things that ever happened to me.

Lexia, Lydia's mom, well—she didn't agree. When she found out about Lydia's autism, her daughter was ruined in her eyes. She wanted nothing to do with her."

"How can she be autistic? Scotty said that she's brilliant."

Staring out toward the ocean, Lee responded, "Lexia found a way to fix her. At the time when she was diagnosed with autism, Dryden's pharmaceutical division happened to be working on an experimental drug for intelligence enhancement, allowing people to utilize the brain's capacity to its fullest. It was really intended to help fight dementia and Alzheimer's disease. Anyway, without my knowing it, Lexia included Lydia with the other humans participating in the testing of this new drug."

"So that's how she became so smart."

"Yeah. Within a few weeks, all signs of her autism disappeared. Her intelligence was off the charts. And by age six—she was considered a genius. But the one thing she wasn't anymore—was my little girl. Everything about her personality changed—and pretty soon we became strangers to each other."

"Is that why she hates you—and me?"

Resting his chin on Sebastian's shoulder, Lee answered with a sigh, "Her hate is one of the side effects of taking the drug. For those who participated in the clinical trial, about two years later each one showed signs of paranoia, aggression, severe panic to the point of suicide, and depression. All attempts to cure or reverse the effects of the drug failed. Of the twenty people injected with it, Lydia was the only one to survive."

After sitting quietly for a few minutes, Sebastian turned to his dad. "We can't stay here, can we?"

"No. That replicate down on the beach won't be the last one to come here."

Sounds coming from somewhere out in the ocean, similar to a moans, startled Sebastian. "What is that?"

Releasing a chuckle, his dad answered, "Those are whales calling out to each other." Taking a deep breath, he added, "Smell that sea breeze."

"I can't," Sebastian confessed, "I can't seem to smell anything, not even dinner tonight."

"How long has it been like that?" his dad asked, his concern clear in his voice.

"A few days now and the tremors are getting stronger," Sebastian revealed further as he studied his hands. "I'm always tired. It's getting worse."

Resting his forehead against Sebastian's, his dad responded, "Then we're going to fight it. I promise."

"How?"

"I have a friend in Montreal who might be able to help. We'll need to sneak across the border—probably end up walking part of the way."

"What if—I can't keep up?" Sebastian nervously asked.

Tenderly pulling him close, his dad whispered in his ear, "Then I'll carry you."

"When should we go?"

Smiling as best he could, his dad answered, "We'll leave at daybreak."

The End

About Jeffery Martin Botzenhart

I've been waiting for you to finish this book. I hope you liked it. So now you want to know about the man who created it, that being me. If you've read other stories by me, then you know you're in for a few minutes of boredom, but let me indulge you anyway since you insist.

I was born in Warren, Ohio in November of 1967 and grew up in a rural trailer park in Southington, Ohio. After graduating high school I attended Kent State University where I earned my Bachelors of Sciences degree in International Relations. It was during my college days that my passion for writing was ignited, though I didn't have my first story published until 2014.

Currently I live in Ohio with my wife and sons. I also love painting and drawing and am a proud coach of soccer for autistic and special needs kids.

Social Media Links:

Facebook:
https://www.facebook.com/jefferymartinbotzenhartwritingjourney/